INTRODUCTION

Pinwheels, Jacob's Ladder, Irish Chain . . . are but a few of the well-known quilt patterns women have been creating for years. "The Quilt Maker" is a collection of stories recorded in this time-honored craft, each told in the quilter's painstaking stitches, the patchwork of characters framed by a pattern.

"**The Quilt Maker** is one of the finest collections of short stories to date. The physical and metaphorical cloth holding each story together provides smiles, nods and tears while it conveys messages of hope, irony and resolution. For a first offering, Barbara Deming did an excellent job and I look forward to more."

> – Harrytru, author of *Icing on Cornbread.*

"Barbara Deming has penned a superb anthology of entertaining, emotional and thought-evoking stories that will touch your heart. Take a journey with the quilt makers through history and nostalgia to the whimsical and the poignant sides of life."

> – Marti Phillips, author of *Angel From The Highlands, The Last Pirate*

The Cover: This colorful "Grandma's Flower Garden" pattern quilt was completely hand stitched and tied by the author's step-daughter, Linda Deming, of Carson City, Nevada.

THE QUILT MAKER

A Short Story Collection

by Barbara Deming

© 2002

ISBN 1-59109-490-9

For inquiries or copies, contact:

Southern Star Publishing

E-mail: BookStarPR@aol.com
Website:
http://hometown.aol.com/Romnovelst/StarBooks.html

For my husband, Ray, who has always encouraged me to write, and to Linda who creates beautiful quilts and shares them with me.

THE QUILTMAKER

By Barbara Deming

Southern Star Publishing
4 Timberline Tr. Box D, Ormond Bch, FL 32174

CONTENTS

PINWHEELS FOR SALE

It was just an old log cabin, unpainted walls, stove chimney rusty and leaning. A porch with railings ran across the front and a wide array of colorful quilts were hanging over the poles. There was no sign, but I had seen them displayed like this all over the Ozarks during my week's stay. After I asked a friendly waitress about these exhibitions, she clued me in on the front-porch sales pitch. I slowly pulled into the gravel driveway beside the cabin. I couldn't resist.

This love for quilts had come from those I had inherited from my grandmother. Mama didn't quilt so couldn't teach me the art, and we moved hundreds of miles away from my grandparents while I was too young to be creative. Later I found that living and working in a city left no time for taking classes for something as frivolous as quilting. It was after the children went away to school and Harry died that I found the time for indulging in my love for the age-old hobby. Now I had hundreds of dollars invested in fabrics, templates, fillers, and threads, not counting the books I collected. The few quilts I made for myself were perfect, or so my instructors told me.

This "perfection" had meant spending hours and hours hunched over a lap frame, pushing through the needle for the daintiest of same-size stitches throughout the design. But if my teachers were right, I often asked myself, why had I never won a prize?

The screened door squeaked as she came out, a tiny woman in a crisp gingham dress almost covered by the floral-printed bib apron.

"Are your quilts for sale?"

Faded blue eyes smiled out of the wrinkled face. "I reckon they are. I'm 'bout to be crowded out of my own house by all of them quilts." She chuckled.

I looked closely at them. They were in numerous colors and patterns, some designs I knew the quilter had created herself, as I had never seen them in any of the pattern books. The stitches weren't even but the overall effect on all of them was lovely. I knew I wanted one. It would be hard to make a choice.

"They're all beautiful." I touched the greens of the Irish Chain pattern.

"Just bits and pieces I've worked together." The look on her face was one of age-old serenity. "My name's Rebecca."

"I'm Deborah." I clasp the worn hand in my soft one.

"Would you like to see some more?" Rebecca held the screen open in invitation.

It took a few minutes for my eyes to adjust to the darkness of the interior. There were quilts on the wall, covering the old sofa, draped across the bed seen through another door. Her quilt frame had been pulled down from the ceiling, anchored by weights hanging off each corner and I could see that she had started still one more quilt.

"This looks like the Shoo Fly pattern."

Rebecca was delighted. "You know your quilts. That's an old Amish pattern."

"I have my grandmother's quilts. One of them is this pattern." I looked around the room. "I've started quilting, too."

"It's a good way to pass the time." She nodded. "Maybe you'd like one of these."

She opened up a cedar chest serving as a coffee table and pulled out a stack of folded quilts in a rainbow of colors. "Just help yourself."

I unfolded them one by one. Morning Glory. Oregon Flower. Sunbonnet Sue. Crazy Patch. Each was as beautiful as the next. Looking closely I found the irregularity of stitches in some places. The binding on some was slightly crooked. There wasn't a perfect one in the bunch.

As I folded the last quilt and prepared to place them back, I saw the ribbons in the bottom of the chest. There must have been a dozen of them, most First Place blues, all from the County Fair. Although not technically perfect, each quilt had been judged artistically best.

"See any you like?" The old woman asked.

"All of them," I answered, then quickly added, "but I can only afford one this trip." I paused before continuing. "I see you've been showing them at fairs."

"Won a good many prizes, I did. Have you entered any of yours?"

"I have but, although my teachers have praised my craftsmanship, I've yet to win a ribbon."

"Why'd you make them?"

"What?" I frowned. "Well, I guess because they were class assignments. Then I entered them in several shows."

"What kind of story was attached?"

"Story?" She was smiling at me. "I don't understand."

"Well, each one of my pieces has a story. See this green and yellow Jacob's Ladder one? I made that for my son-in-law. By and by, my daughter died, then later he remarried, thought it should be returned to me. That Broken Star was done with my husband's old work shirts. The bright red and blue patchwork was made for my Don when he was real sick with meningitis."

"What about the Pinwheel one?"

Tears welled in her eyes as she rubbed her hand up and down the quilt. "My mother was the best quilter in the county. Next to her quilts, she treasured her cut glass. I think they call it Depression glass now. The pinwheel pattern was the one she liked best. She went blind while still pretty young and before too long was bedridden. I made this quilt for her to use then."

"How can you sell them?"

"Can't hold on to past days. I'm makin' ones with new stories now." She peered at me closely. "I'm of a mind that your quilts don't win ribbons because they have no stories to tell. Where do you get your material?"

"I purchase most of it from a shop that specializes in quilting fabrics."

"Why that's just some man makin' up fancy cloth to sell." She laughed. "You have to use your own scraps. Pieces from curtains you made for the kitchen, some from that fancy dress you wore one special Christmas long ago or the jeans you finally stopped wearin' because they had too many holes to be decent. Those scraps tell a story, see?"

I nodded. Rebecca pulled out another quilt from an old pine dresser. Though in different textures, it was all made of white pieces, the pattern etched in ivory-colored quilting stitches, interlaced hearts forming rings in each block.

"This one, not for sale mind you, has lots of tales to tell. The background is the train from my daughter's wedding dress. The baskets are made of christening gowns used by our relatives from way back. These here are from the granddaughter's graduation dresses. There's a past to this quilt that you could never find with new cloth."

I knew then why my quilts had never won. Though perfectly stitched on the best of fabrics with hours of work in each one, the pieces I had created had no love sewn into them. My quilts had no heart.

"Better decide on one," Rebecca urged.

* * *

Today, on one wall of my living room hangs the Pinwheel-patterned quilt Rebecca sold me that day. Opposite it is my own Sunshine and Shadows. Hanging from one edge is my first blue ribbon. Made from scraps I had found in my mother's belongings, fabrics from both her past and mine, with stitches done long and wide and sometimes not straight, it was the most perfectly love-made piece I had ever created.

~

SUNSHINE AND SHADOWS

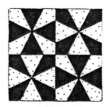

"Those women of ours are out of control," Jim continued the conversation interrupted by Vera refilling their coffee cups. "Amelia's never home."

"Lois never has time to bake my favorite apply pie any- more," Claude complained.

"Before she got involved with that quiltin' circle, Maude was always an extra hand in the fields. Now, she says I should retire anyway and, if not, I can just hire someone to fill in."

Homer's tone begged for sympathy even before he asked, "What can we do?"

"We could put our foot down," Claude offered. "Tell them they've got to spend more time at home."

"Oh, yeah, and who's goin' to save you when Lois lets you have it, Claude? You know she's gonna do what she dern well pleases, same as the others." Jim said, shaking his head as the others mumbled their sentiments. "All those women would quit cookin' for sure, lock the bedroom door, then the whole blamed town would be notified that we're tryin' to take away their independence."

"Could we shut the funds off so they couldn't buy all that material and stuff?" Homer asked.

"Heck, Homer," Claude cut in, "Lois has an inheritance from her Daddy that would buy all the supplies the whole quiltin' circle could ever need from here to Kingdom Come! Besides, our wives are partners in all the farms. There's no way we could leave and make them penniless."

The men shook their heads in silence, as there seemed no way out of their bind. Then Jim spoke softly. "We could give them some competition."

"What do ya mean?" Claude asked, suspiciously.

"We could form our own circle."

"You mean a fishin' group or somethin' like that?" Homer asked.

"No, Homer, I mean real competition."

"Well, we sure can't quilt." Homer laughed.

"Why not?"

"Are you crazy, Jim? Men don't quilt!" Claude bellowed.

"Who says? There are some pretty macho men who crochet and do needlepoint."

"Yeah, but nobody's gonna question someone as big as Rosie Greer when he drags out his needles," Claude observed, then added, "I wouldn't know where to begin."

"We can learn." Jim said, then went on to outline the plan that had been formulating in his head for the past couple of days.

"That all sounds like sissy stuff to me, Jim," Homer protested after Jim finished. "What's the point?"

"Well, the county fair's comin' up," Jim continued, "and the women are working on an entry. That means even more hours away from us. To begin with, our circle will meet on the days they decide they'll be at home. That will give them a taste of what it's like to be sittin' there."

"That's the competition?"

"The time we aren't around is only part of it. The next thing we zap them with is the quilt we'll enter in the fair."

"Us!" Homer yelped. "Are you serious?"

"It'll never work," Claude predicted.

But they all agreed they had to do something. So the next few days, the three men traveled to Clayton to take a basic class. They didn't want the women to have any idea what they were really doing in their "circle," so they decided to go out of town.

Maude, Lois, and Amelia were a little put out when they came home to empty houses, with no one to tell the latest gossip. When they asked their men where they were off to, they were told each had joined a new club called "Hitchin' Time." When they tried to get more information out of their odd-behaving husbands, all three clammed up, saying it was a secret men's organization. Weeks of this went by, and the women grew more and more disturbed. After all, between their quilting circle and this mysterious men's group, the couples were seldom home at the same time.

As Lois poured hot tea for her friends at the dining room table one afternoon, she announced. "We never even have lunch together anymore. What is going on with them?"

"I seem to remember you were too busy for lunch or baking," Amelia reminded her.

"Homer used to ask me to ride to the fields with him, and help out once in awhile. He doesn't even talk about the crops anymore," Maude said.

"Didn't you tell him to retire, or hire someone to help out?" Amelia asked.

"Well, Jim told Homer you were never home for anything anymore, so don't play 'Miss Goody-Two-Shoes' with us, Amelia Burleson," Lois pointed out, rather sharply.

"Girls, we'll just have to worry about this after the fair. Just a few more days stitching, and we'll be finished with our entry," Maude said calmly.

By opening day, the couples were hardly speaking to each other. It was so bad that Maude, Lois, and Amelia set off by themselves to the fair for the quilt judging. Their husbands had left earlier for breakfast at the coffee shop and another of their "secret" meetings. Ever since their courting days, they had always attended the county fair as couples. It was enough to make anyone upset, but certainly not enough to miss the quilting competition.

There was a large crowd gathered in the building housing the craft exhibits; artwork, photography and needlework. As most women tend to do, Maude, Lois, and

Amelia began at the beginning to see it all. The nearer they got to the quilt display, the thicker the crowd became. When they finally spotted their Wedding Ring-pattern, they cheered.

"A red ribbon, girls!" Lois shouted, gathering them close for a hug. "That's better than last year. We'll just have to keep trying for that blue."

"I wonder who got the 'Best of Show'?" Maude asked, glancing around.

Amelia moved into a tight group gathered in front of the last display. When she finally broke through, she saw a wall hanging done in the Sunshine and Shadow pattern. With browns and golds in a design that resembled a plowed field, it was familiar to any quilter, but this one had a unique feature. At the edge of every fourth was an appliquéd green tractor. The brand names, John Deere, Allis-Chalmers, and International Harvester were stitched on the individual machines.

Amelia couldn't believe the scene before her. It took several tries before she finally found her voice and she reached out to pull Maude and Lois into the circle. "You've got to see this," she finally stammered.

Standing beside the quilt, holding their blue ribbon in front of them, were Jim, Claude, and Homer. The three women pushed forward. "What's going on, Jim?" Amelia growled, hands on her hips.

"What are you doing with that ribbon?" Maude followed.

"Claude, get that silly grin off your face," Lois commanded. "We demand an explanation right this very minutes!"

Suddenly everyone was talking at once. Soon it was all sorted out, and the "secret" group unfolded. The "Hitchin' and Stitchin'" circle had won the blue ribbon for their creative interpretation of an old favorite pattern. With their instructor's help, the men had made the quilt unique with its addition of tractors to symbolize the farms they all came from

"We decided there was nothing else we could do," Jim explained. If you can't change 'em, join 'em! We were getting pretty lonesome before all this started."

The woman could only look guiltily at each other, realizing they had started all of this. They had gotten carried away with their own quilting. It had become the most important thing of their days. How long had it been since they had listened to the highlights of their husbands' day? Baked their favorite dessert? Taken a late afternoon stroll through the fields?

"We understand, fellows," Maude admitted. "Let's make a pact here and now. We'll bake, we'll walk with you, we'll help when needed, we'll share our time. We promise to keep our Circle meetings to a minimum, if you will promise to do one thing."

The men beamed. "What can we do?"

In unison, the women quipped, "Stop quilting! We want that blue ribbon next year!"

~

TEDDY BEAR'S PICNIC

"I'll make a quilt for his first birthday." I can still hear the excitement in his mother's voice, so young then.

"I'll appliqué, Teddy bears in the corner of each block. I think the pattern is sometimes called 'Teddy Bear's Picnic.' Michael will love it."

* * *

I know I'll find the door to Trent's Funeral Home open this morning no matter how early I arrive. Jim Trent agreed to my request when I called last night, almost as if he had been waiting for it. He made sure that I could have some time with Michael before they move the casket to the church.

There is a light dusting of new snow that has fallen over-night. It's turned icy and I find myself walking more slowly toward the center of town. Maybe it's a good thing; it gives me some time to collect my thoughts. Bundled up, the small package tucked in my parka pocket, my rambling mind touches on everything from days past as Michael grew up to the difference between the heat and burning sun of a Saudi Arabian winter and the one he had always known in his hometown. *Was it easier to die there?*

The side door to Trent's is open. I quickly move to the viewing room we chose. It's cold. Maybe to keep the dozens of floral arrangements at their best, or, possibly it is because Michael has no need for heat.

I know they closed the casket last night after the final viewing. Jim opened it again for me. I'm glad. It takes almost all of the strength I have to walk across the room and face my son, something more from deep inside me to speak.

"There are things I should have said to you, Michael. So many times I wanted to but I let the opportunity slip by. I've been praying about this, knowing in my heart that it was too late. I asked God to forgive me for my omissions and maybe He will grant me the wish that by some miracle you can hear me." I don't attempt to wipe away the tears.

"You need to know, son, how proud we are of you. Desert Storm wasn't an easy assignment. We felt such relief when you were finally at your post and we heard your voice. Your mother didn't want me to know but of course I did, that she was much more worried over this thing than any of the other skirmishes. People say to rely on your faith in hard times. Your mother and I prayed more than we had in years.

I had hoped you'd never go to war. My father thought he had fought the last one in France. Your uncle left a leg on Guadalcanal. I hung onto the open door of the last helicopter out of Saigon. Then you, someone who didn't have to be exposed to these chances, decided the Army was the career you wanted. It just about killed your mother, son, but she would never tell you.

Of course, I didn't say much about it either except at first when I told you how crazy it was to join up. I'm sorry for those words, son, for you made an excellent soldier. I should have said so long before now. Why was it always so hard for me to tell you how I felt? From the day you were born, you were my boy, my tagalong partner, my fishing buddy. Then you hit those teenage years and we never seemed to agree on anything. Why didn't you do your chores without being told? Did we need a hassle before you got a haircut? Couldn't you drive without squealing your tires? Why didn't you sign up for the football team? Or college? And why couldn't I let you be the young man you wanted to be?

I'm glad we talked some the last time you came home. It was time I admitted that you had an opinion worthy of listening to. We had both grown up enough to respect each other, because no matter what, we loved each other, didn't we, Michael?"

I take the package out, clutch the frayed piece of cloth in my shaking hands, crumble the brown paper and shove it into my coat pocket.

"Do you remember your quilt, son, the one with the Teddy bears? You took that quilt everywhere, wouldn't settle down to sleep without it. When your bottle was taken away, you put a corner of the quilt over your thumb as you sucked yourself to sleep. Your mother said it was your security blanket. I made it plain that no son of mine was going to be a sissy. Little men weren't supposed to suck their thumb or drag around a blanket. But every time I took it away you protested so long and loud I was forced to give it back in order to get a good night's sleep.

As usual, your mother had the solution. Square by square she cut off pieces, making your security blanket smaller and smaller. By your fourth birthday there was only one block left. And your mother told you that Santa had taken the pretty piece in exchange for a bright red tricycle. No cloth, no thumb sucking.

That wasn't the first or the last time she was right about you and me. Somehow your mother always understood all of those tugs of war we had would one day be forgotten by both of us. We did forget all of our differences, didn't we, Michael.

I know now that we all need something symbolic to hold on to, something or someone that makes us feel safe and secure and happy. I wish I had the whole quilt to wrap you in but this will have to do."

It isn't easy, tucking the last Teddy Bear block beneath the hardened folded hands but somehow I manage. I lean over to kiss the smooth, cold cheek. Seeing Michael's face through fresh tears, I close the casket lid for the last time.

Taking our nation's security blanket, the flag bearing the bright stars and wide stripes, I very carefully cover my son's eternal bed.

~

JACOB'S LADDER

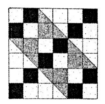

As the bus pulled out of the station, a lone passenger stood there. The Army uniform looked stiff with the regulation creases. On the left breast of the shirt hung several ribbons and medals, the sharpshooter badge being the only one I recognized. Above the solemn dark face, fixed just at the proper angle above dark eyes, was the pointed campaign cap. I was sure if I could see them, I would have been able to apply my lipstick in the shine on his shoes. From his clothing to the erect bearing, the figure before me was a soldier and proud of it.

When he still stood after several miles of holding onto the rack over our heads, swaying on the curves, and changing the gripping hand from time to time, I looked up at him with a puzzled expression.

"Aren't you going to sit down?"

"Couldn't do that, ma'am."

"Why ever not?"

"It wouldn't be proper." He looked at me with a frown. "You're a young white lady."

I was raised in a small Southern town where in the 1950's, of course, there had been a division of the people who lived there. My parents had never heard of "civil rights" at the time, but they had brought all of their children up with the belief that God created all creatures, and none of them, no matter what color, was to be treated with anything less than kindness and respect. I had no idea of any special rules regarding people of color. Rather naive, even for those times, I must admit. So I innocently smiled at him, and patted the seat next to me.

"Well, I don't know much about what's supposed to be proper but it's certainly not right for a soldier to stand all the way to Atlanta."

He hesitated for a moment, shoved a small bag on the floor beneath his feet, then sat down as close to the aisle as he could. The silence stretched on as darkness enclosed the bus. Others went to sleep, but we both sat upright.

"My name's Jeannette." I finally spoke, in a low voice. "Are you going home?"

"I'm Jim, and, yes, I'm going home to a small town just south of Atlanta," he answered after a short pause. "And you?"

"I've been caring for an aunt in Richmond. She's better now, so I'm headed home."

"Where's home?"

And we continued to talk, very quietly so as not to disturb our fellow passengers. Or maybe it was really because deep inside we felt we should speak to each other in secret. Whatever the reason, it was enjoyable to share tales of my town and family with him, and it was interesting to learn that he had been given a ten-day pass to visit his mother before he left. She was "down," as he put it, and . . . well, you never knew what would happen if this thing in Cuba led to war, did you?

Breakfast was served family style for the passengers early in the morning at a small café somewhere in North Carolina. We sleepily stumbled up to tables laden with plates of scrambled eggs, bowls of steaming grits, a platter of spicy sausage, and mounds of hot biscuits.

I started to follow Jim, when he stopped, and sharply whispered to me. "Don't! Go over there with the others."

"What?" I was suddenly very awake.

"I'm not allowed to eat with whites." He spit out, though still in a low voice. When he saw what must have been shock on my face, he softened. "I don't know what kind of town you grew up in, Jeannette, but it's not the real world. Go now. I don't want to see you hurt."

We were both more subdued for many miles after breakfast. I was lost in thought, beginning to understand how sheltered I had been, how cruel the world actually was. How could one group of people think themselves so superior to another? And it was accepted, too. That made it even more disgusting.

I was the one who once again sought out conversation. "What do you do in your hometown? I mean, before you joined the Army?"

He didn't hesitate this time. "I joined up right out of high school. You mean, for fun? I played music."

"Really. Jazz? Blues?"

He laughed. "Would you believe western swing?"

I was surprised. "Like Bob Wills?"

"Like Bob Wills, but not as good."

"What instrument did you play? Did you have a band? Where did you play?"

"I play steel guitar with a small group. We played for birthdays and weddings, and sometimes at a club in Atlanta."

The afternoon flew by as we discussed music and art (he liked seascapes, too), and books we had read. I remember thinking what an interesting young man he was. But the niceness was wiped out when we stopped for dinner that night. The bus driver and an older lady pulled me aside.

"Uh, we've been noticing that colored boy seems to be bothering you, miss."

"Bothering me?" I shook my head. "Oh, no, we're just talking about families and growing up. It passes time, you know."

"Well, it's unladylike for you to be talking with him." The white-haired woman blurted out, anger echoed in her voice and cold blue eyes. "You'll get a bad reputation, young lady."

"We're just trying to protect you since your parents aren't around." The bus driver added.

I could feel my face turning red. "My parents would be very disappointed in me if I acted any differently toward this soldier, no matter what color."

"Then they're nigger lovers, too," the venomous woman spat.

I'd never heard the phrase. By the ugly tone, I understood its meaning. I bristled, "We love everybody, even the small minded."

When I returned to the bus, Jim looked at me sympathetically, as if he understood what had happened. Stubborn child that I had always been, we were barely seated before I asked, "Is your mother too ill to meet you in Atlanta?"

Jim turned to me, surprise written on his face. It was some time before he answered. "She's too crippled up with arthritis in her knees." He chuckled. "It's a good thing it's not in her hands."

"Why's that?"

"She loves to quilt. Mama would just about die if she couldn't make those quilts. Gives most of them away now. It's her way of thanking people for little . . . or big . . . kindnesses." He pulled the bag from beneath his feet. "She never wants a gift - just find her more material for her quilts, she always says."

He unrolled colorful fabric to show me. Jim could even name some of the patterns she created . . . Wedding Ring, Dresden Plate, Nine Patch. When he pulled out the soft white wool and then another roll of shiny black satin, he grimaced.

"She's found this new pattern, something called Jacob's Ladder. She asked me to bring home some cloth in black and white. Do you think this will do?"

I touched the fabrics. "My granny made quilts out of

everything. Nothing as elegant as wool and satin though. I'm sure this will make a lovely piece."

In the Atlanta bus terminal, one of the first things I noticed was the signs. Had they been there before and, if so, was I so engrossed in my own life that I was blind to the hypocrisy? WHITE ONLY painted over the restrooms. COLORED over one water fountain. WHITE over the other. I stood there waiting for a transfer, feeling ashamed of the chasm looming between us. I also noticed the acid-tongued woman watching. Possibly more confident on his home ground, Jim extended his hand to me.

I looked down for a moment at my small slender hand engulfed by his large dark one. It was almost a shock to realize how different our skins were. Is that what the signs were about?

"Thank you, Jeannette. You were a great traveling partner."

"I enjoyed it, Jim. Give your mother my best wishes." I smiled, a little sad at the exchange of farewells. "I'll remember you in my prayers."

I shared the story of Jim with my family and over the next few weeks thought often of the young soldier. I gave thanks to the heavens when the Russians backed down and none of the soldiers, including Jim, had to face an enemy. I was busy with a new job, college classes, even a new relationship. The large package that arrived at the post office one summer day was quite unexpected.

Ruth Johnson was the name on the return address, followed by a familiar town in Georgia. So that was his last name, I thought, as I tore the letter off the front of the package. It began with greetings and apologies for taking so long to thank me for the compassionate treatment of her son.

"I always try to do a little something to repay my friends for the kindness that is unasked for and certainly unexpected. I hope you will enjoy this as my thanks . . ."

Pulling the contents out of the package, I gasped as I saw the black and white fabric. Unfolding the quilt, I marveled at the beauty of the black satin squares and triangles with a scattering of burgundy diamonds as highlights. The entire effect on the white wool background presented a complete interlocking of pattern and shapes. The purple border gave it a touch of spirit that lifted the complementary black and white colors. It was truly lovely.

As I gently touched the intricate stitches, in my memory I could once again see those hands, black and white, forever clasped in understanding.

~

LIBERTY STAR

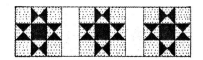

The tests are back, Millie." Dr. Ed Barnes sat in a chair next to me. "It's malignant."

I wasn't really shocked. I seemed to have known that the fuzzy spot on the mammogram, too small to be felt, too large to wait for the next annual test, would be cancerous.

He continued. "I've reviewed it by phone with the pathologist, and we're both sure it's self-contained."

"But you really won't know until you get in there, will you?" I gripped my hands together tightly, trying to hold fast to the rising fear that wanted to leap out.

"Not fully, but I've spoken to the surgeon, too, and he's proposing a lumpectomy with removal of four lymph nodes. That means he's not worried that it's spread either."

"If this was your wife, Dottie, what would you suggest?"

"The same, Millie." I could hear the enthusiasm as he continued. "East Memorial Hospital in Portland has the best cancer treatment center in the Northwest. They're doing amazing things with cases of advanced cancer, and yours is so small. One of their top surgeons has been in all the medical journals, and he's asked to be your surgeon."

I frowned. "Asked? Why would he do that?"

Ed laughed. "Heck if I know. When I spoke with him, he said he had a debt to repay."

"What does that have to do with my surgery?"

Ed shook his head. "Your mysterious Dr. Terrell said to tell you he's still number one."

"Terrell? Peter Terrell?" When he nodded, I sank back in my chair. "Oh, my."

"He's supposed to be a whiz at cutting cancers out, Millie." He wanted me to feel confident with the choice of a surgeon. Ed couldn't know how much more comfortable I suddenly felt.

"He'll be fine, Ed. When do I go in?"

"I tentatively accepted June 10, a week from tomorrow. You'll go up the night before. It's a simple procedure. With no unforeseen problem, you'll be home the next day with a small drain that I'll remove in about seven days. Dottie says she's ready to see the grand kids again and will drive you up and back."

Later, a hot bath took all of the kinks out of my treacherous body that felt so healthy, though tired, so unmarked on the surface. After a light dinner, I moved into the den to set up the latest quilt I had started. Tightening the rollers at the edge of the large frame, I began to sew. The blocks of the multicolored quilt were done with in-the-ditch stitches and, after doing so many of them on this piece, my mind could wander.

No matter what anyone tells you, teachers have favorite kids in their classrooms. They also have that one special student that drives them to distraction. I was no different from the other educators, especially the young ones. Peter Terrell was a student that I disliked from the very first day he entered my class. Not only was he, at fourteen, a year older and much taller than the others, he was the class clown, drawing laughter at the most inopportune moments. With only a year of experience teaching, I wasn't too accepting of behavior problems.

He wore the same jeans for weeks. Didn't his mother ever wash clothes, or was he just as uncaring as he seemed? He never had a fresh haircut. Surely his father could take him to Sam for a cut to control that wild mop of black curls. There was no such thing as him doing homework, and Peter did poorly on the class work, too. Instead of listening, he would whisper some funny comment, or when my back was turned he would make outlandish faces for the attention it always received from his classmates. Then came the day he failed to turn in his Science project.

"Peter Terrell, I have had enough." My voice almost shook with the anger I felt. I'm sending notice to your parents to meet with me for a conference."

"It won't do any good." Though Peter spoke belligerent-ly, I was stopped for a moment by the flash of fear in his voice.

"Then I shall make a trip out to see them."

"Please, don't, Miss Brewster." I was beyond hearing the anguish in his voice.

"You have to learn, Peter, that there are consequences when we don't accept our responsibilities."

"It won't help none to see my Pa."

That turned out to be the understatement of the day. Homer Terrell seemed to not care at all if his son misbehaved, and cared even less for teachers who snooped into his business, as he bluntly put it. He disliked any teacher who showed up at his door. He stubbornly stood in the doorway, never inviting me in so that we might discuss a way to make Peter more receptive to the art of learning. Through the doorway I could see clothes and newspapers strewn about the room and, beyond, a dingy-looking cat sat on the table licking dishes left there.

Peter wasn't at school the next day. He had never missed and it made me feel uneasy. When I spoke of the situation at lunch in the teachers lounge, the sixth grade teacher, Pam Ballard, turned to me, shock etched on her face.

"Don't you realize what you've done? Homer Terrell has always been a rotten father, a drunk for years. When his wife died, there was no buffer between him and Peter."

I could feel the bile rise in my throat as I remembered my own father's rages when he was drunk. "Does he abuse his son?"

"What do you think?"

"Oh, God, forgive me."

Two days later Peter returned with a yellowing bruise on his cheek, and stiffness in his walk. That was the afternoon we sat in my room after classes to talk, to really talk. I told him about my father, the terror he caused my family. Peter told me, not about the physical abuse I knew he suffered but about being shut out of the house most nights, told to sleep in the barn with the animals.

From then on I worked with him on lessons; sometimes he just stayed to do homework while I graded papers. He came to school with his hair trimmed and combed, and his jeans were always washed. How he managed, I never asked, as I knew it would embarrass him to know that I had noticed. Most of the clowning was reserved for the hallways. And we never spoke of our common nightmares again.

Before winter arrived I completed a gift for Peter. The "Liberty Star" patterned quilt was done in bright reds and midnight blues, and was large enough for a tall boy to roll up in. It was all I could do to hold back my tears when I watched the look of amazement flood his face as I unfolded it for him to view.

"It will keep you warm." I dared not mention the cold barn.

Peter's eyes were shining. "It's the most beautiful thing I've ever seen. It's really for me?"

"Just for you." I smiled at the gangly boy clutching the quilt to his chest. "Who knows? It might have magic powers."

He grinned. "Like good grades? Or college?"

I shook my head. "No, Peter, you don't need this quilt for that. You'll create your own magic."

And he had. Peter graduated to high school second in his class. When he was chosen valedictorian four years later, he called to give me the news that he was "numero uno," as he called the honor. The card I received four years later said he was in the top ten graduates of his college, still "numero uno, Miss Brewster."

I had continued making my quilts, and, as my eyes and heart had been opened, I always found a special student that needed a spot of warmth and brightness in their life. Though I hadn't heard from Peter for some time--didn't know that he had become a doctor until now--each time I gave one of my quilts away I remembered him with fondness. It would be wonderful to see him again, even under these circumstances.

In the hospital I was restless until the dinner tray was removed. I wandered up and down the halls, watched some television in the lounge with visitors, and then stopped by the nurse's station to inquire about my surgeon's schedule.

"Dr. Terrell will see you on his rounds after seven." She smiled up at me. "You sure lucked out getting him. He's tops."

Settled back in my room, tucked into bed, it was a faint rustle of paper that made me aware of his presence in the room. Scrub greens covered the tall, filled out body. He held himself so straight and it was with pleasure that I noticed the air of confidence that oozed out of him. But I almost laughed at the tangle of curls that topped this important figure. There was still some of the boy from the past left, after all.

"When I read the case history, I knew I had to take care of you, Teach." He grinned, warm brown eyes feeding me assurance. "I promise to do a good job tomorrow."

"You always did, Peter." I squeezed the fingers curled around mine. "How wonderful to see you again. Do you have time to talk, to tell me all about yourself?"

"I saved you for last on my rounds so we could do just that." He pulled the chair up to the edge of the bed.

For the next thirty minutes, Peter told me all about the years in medical school that he had sailed through, loving every long stretch of duty. He had married a young nurse he met while an intern and just two months before they had welcomed a son into their world. What a great life Peter had created out of bad times, hard work, and determination. I rejoiced in his success. It was not often that teachers know what happens to their students who shove off into the tumultuous world beyond their hometowns. Too often when they do hear, it's about the ones involved in crimes, accidents, or death. How good it felt to have been a small part of Peter's success story.

He rose, shoved the chair back in its place, and reached for the package he had left near the door. When he unfolded it, I was stunned to see the "Liberty Star" quilt, patched in several places, its colors now faded.

"This quilt has kept me safe and warm through many struggles," he said as he tucked it around me. "I thought you might need its magic tonight."

"Oh, Peter . . ." Tears were close to spilling over.

"It's only a loan, mind you." He shook his finger at me. "You won't be needing it for long because you've got me, "numero uno" surgeon. Besides . . ." Peter leaned over to kiss my cheek, "my son will have lessons to learn, too, lessons that only the story of this quilt can teach. See you tomorrow, Teach."

~

GRANDMOTHER'S DREAM

Aunt Ada had died. Everyone had been notified. All said they would come since she had the good sense to wait until April to die, when the winter storms were over. Travel in the late 1800's hadn't improved much since some of the members of the family had crossed the plains in the early years of our century but all that counted made the trip.

Jasper is a small town and had only one hotel worth staying in. Our relatives took every available room. That left three of the cousins squeezed into the one spare room at the family home. Granny, who had never expected to outlive any of her children, used a daybed in the small room she called her study. My parents, who had traveled several hundred miles suffering from exhaustion, took over Aunt Ada's room. I, arriving by train from Baltimore Women's College, slept under my aunt's favorite creation, a quilt done in bright reds and golds that she called "Grandmother's Dream." My aunt always believed that quilt, with its pattern of wide pieces formed in a cross with diamonds in the center and at each corner of the block, had a special touch to it. She had claimed it was a miracle quilt, whatever that was supposed to mean. *It hadn't helped her much.* Aunt Ada was lying in the parlor.

"Maggie, people will be coming to pay their respects soon." Granny stood over me as I curled up on the settee that had been moved into a corner of the dining room. "The area must be made ready and you need to prepare Ada for viewing."

"Oh, no." Although she was my favorite aunt I wasn't yet comfortable with Aunt Ada's demise, certainly not with having a close encounter with her body. "Wouldn't you rather do this yourself, Granny?"

"No. . .no, I just couldn't." Her faded gray eyes filled with tears as she hurried back to the security of her kitchen.

Because they didn't embalm, the custom was to lay the dead out in the parlor for a day or so, and then have a quick burial. It became my duty to remove the veil from the coffin lid that had shielded Aunt Ada since she had been placed in the fancy satin-lined box. My hands shook as I lifted, then folded up, the cloth. It was hard to think that the vivacious, nonconformist female who had taught me what little independence I could manage to grasp, would never again be there for me when I came back from a semester of college, or in from a date with some dashing beau she just must hear all about.

"You look lovely, Aunt Ada," I whispered as I looked down at her. "I choose your favorite gray crepe dress, the one you always wore on special occasions. I'm sure you would have worn it on the day I graduated college. And to my wedding one day."

I straightened the white collar, her favorite pearl broach, the one shaped like a swan, pinned to it. Matching pearls graced the ears she always thought too small for the fashionable heavy jewelry. Aunt Ada had always been fastidious with her grooming. For that reason, I had been the one to take her best dress to the undertaker and make sure that he called in her favorite hairdresser.

"Miss Lucy did your hair just perfect, Aunt Ada." She looked so natural as she lay there, like she'd simply fallen asleep for a nap." "You're missing a beautiful spring, you know. The wisteria shows almost solid purple on the arbor today. Those rose bushes we put in the ground on New Year's Day have filled out with shiny red-green leaves on long runners. And those daffodils you planted along the walk are opening in the warm sunshine."

Sadness surrounded the room as I realized that she could no longer feel the morning sun as it filtered through the parlor blinds. Her body would be cold, frozen in death that had come too soon. A new sickness had spread across the country, sending people into a deep coma-like sleep that often quickly led to death. My dear Aunt Ada had been caught in its grip.

I thought I had cleansed myself of all the grief but as I reached into the coffin and touched her folded hands, a single tear slipped down my cheek. Then something sifted through my subconscious, beginning faintly, then really grabbing my senses. I jerked my hand back in shock. I could feel my heart pump wildly in my bosom. Fear grasped me, then shock. I made myself reach out and touch Aunt Ada's hand once more.

It was warm. Her hand was warm!

At the sound of my screams, everyone came running into the room. Granny shook my shoulders when no one could understand my almost-hysterical ramblings. When she finally understood me, Granny sent for the mirrors. Then the others also shrieked as they watched the fog appear on the glass.

Dr. Hadley was blamed for signing a false certificate of death. The undertaker was defamed for not properly preparing a supposedly dead body for burial. The food was sent back to the neighbors. Relatives left in a huff because this special occasion had amounted to nothing. Aunt Ada was the most confused of all.

"What am I doing in my best frock? With my pearl jewelry no less! It's not Tuesday, is it? I always have my hair done on Tuesdays." She grumbled as I helped her into her flannel nightgown. "And what were all of those relatives doing here? You'd think someone had died or something."

As she climbed into bed, Aunt Ada cast a piercing look on me. "Now, missy, you just go get my quilt right now. I don't know what you're doing with it, but that's my very favorite of all the ones I've made and, by golly, you can't have it until I am dead and buried. You hear?"

Pulling the quilt under her chin, Aunt Ada swore she was never going to sleep again as too many peculiar things went on when she wasn't awake. She had to keep an eye on things.

~

CROSS AND CROWN

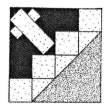

I never knew my father. Three months after I was born on a cold April day in 1945, he was blown up in Rittershoffen, a small town in a part of France that had once been Germany. Mother only said that he had been a wonderful young man. If his letters were any indication, he *was* a special man. She let me read them and he wrote of his love for her, how proud he was to have a daughter, what a great life it was going to be when he returned.

One of those letters had been written to me, the baby he'd never see. The V-mail piece was tucked into a scrapbook with the only picture I had, one of those usual sepia-toned jobs with him decked out in dress uniform, the one that was now packed in mothballs in the attic.

Dear Nancy,

What a pretty name your mother chose for you. She tells me you have my red hair and her smile. Isn't your mother the prettiest mommy any little girl could ever want? Or that any daddy could be lucky enough to call wife? If you grow up to be just like her, you can expect to be a very special woman.

I'm carrying a memento from her, something she made with those pretty soft hands she touches you with. It's a small quilt. . . well, I think mommy would call it more a small group of blocks, the beginning of a quilt she has promised to finish when I bring this home. The pattern's something called 'Cross and Crown'. I guess the cross is for Jesus, maybe the crown, too. Or maybe crowns for us all when we get back. I often roll it up to use for my pillow when we're on the move. I think it sort of protects me. I do know that it's a piece of home that's become a world traveler - England, France, Germany soon

I'll bring it home to you, Baby Girl, and it will keep you safe, too.

Your Daddy Mike

Michael Talbot didn't return to us and our life hadn't been the wonderful one he had promised. Mother worked long hours to provide for the two of us. She didn't have much time or stamina to answer those questions I always had. Or maybe, when I look back, she just couldn't bring back what few memories she had.

The quilt didn't return either. Mother said she had been too grief-stricken to worry about something so unimportant as a piece of cloth. In her youth, and even while she waited my birth, she had pieced and stitched several quilts; two of them were used in the bedroom I grew up in, one covered the threadbare sofa in the living room, another small one hung like a painting in the entryway.

Daddy's death seemed to squelch her love for quilt making. She never made another one.

Sam couldn't understand my sudden need to learn everything I could about my father.

"Sam, you always had your family intact. Mine was always missing a father. When I first entered school and everyone talked about what their father did, I used to pretend that he was away, somewhere at sea, never home. Later, I just said he was dead. Period. That ended the conversation."

"Didn't your mother talk about him?"

"Very seldom. My grandmother told me what he was like as a boy, how my folks met, that sort of thing. She was the one who told me how he died."

"Surely you and your mother spoke of him at the hospital."

"We tried. I don't know if she had forgotten because of her illness, or if she felt she had nothing more to offer. She said they had been married only two years when he was shipped out, not enough time to build a lot of moments that would cling to her memory. She didn't seem to be able to tell me much about the man I've wanted to cherish."

"But, honey, what can I do to help?" Sam was at a loss to what I needed. I wasn't so sure that I had an answer for him either.

I was more than a little put out with myself. Most people would think it pretty pathetic when a fifty-five year old woman is this needy for the least bit of information about a man who had died half a century ago. But I couldn't stop this.

Several months later, on Veteran's Day, I attended memorial services at a nearby National Cemetery as I had been doing for years. Here, especially among the honored dead, I always felt the closest to my Daddy. My eyes swept the crowd, picking out the men who wore Army caps or insignias, wanting to question them, embarrassed that I didn't have the right words. It was then that the guest speaker's voice pierced my thoughts.

"So, if you've lost someone in World War II and have a computer, you should join Gwen's on-line support group."

At the close of his address, I made my way through the crowd to the Colonel's side. Standing quietly while men spoke with him about places they had served, buddies they had lost, I waited until the last one moved away.

"Colonel, I wonder if I might have the web site you spoke of?"

"Sure." He pulled out a business card and wrote on the back. "You lost someone in the War?"

"Yes. my father. I. . . I never knew him, and my mother . . . well, she . . ." I hesitated for a moment, then went on to tell the Colonel my story.

When I finished, he touched my arm gently. "I'm sure Gwen can help you, Nancy. Don't put it off."

The web site showed me how to send for my father's records from a center in St. Louis. It listed phone numbers of military organizations and unit reunions. My heart pounded at the idea that I could actually speak to men who had known him.

Of course, the government doesn't work very fast. It was spring before I received a large brown envelope from St. Louis. I sat on the floor using the large glass coffee table as a desk to pour over the papers. In the next twenty minutes I learned more about my Daddy than anyone had ever told me.

He was born on December 10, 1925. *Heavens, with my birthday on the 12th we'd have had one grand party each year, wouldn't we have?* He had been six feet tall and, at 150 pounds, very slender. He'd finished two years of college, majoring in journalism and baseball. . . *baseball?* . . . and had recently married Marie Callahan of Tulsa when Uncle Sam came calling.

I learned he rode horses and puttered at keeping his jalopy running. His favorite pastime had been hiking the Ozarks. I grew up loving to tramp the woods and mountains, never imagining that we might have walked some of the same paths.

By December of 1944, Lt. Talbot had finished his training and had landed in Marseilles, France when the Battle of the Bulge swallowed him up. There was a copy of the standard letter, a letter Mother never shared with me, maybe one she never kept. "It is with deep regret that your Government informs you of the death of . . ."

A document listed the possessions that were returned; packets of letters, a folder of photos, a pocketknife, the

Army-issue watch...few items left from a man whose face her Mother may have already been finding hard to remember. *I wonder what she did with his stuff?*

After I received a roster of Daddy's battalion, I ran my fingers down the list until I found his Company's section. Several of the men lived in or around Tulsa. But I couldn't dial the numbers, afraid none of these men would remember Mike Talbot.

I prayed for the courage to pick up the phone.

God led me to James Woodbridge in Muskogee. When he came on the line my hands were sweating as I stumbled through my story. Jim chuckled, when I paused.

"You sound just like your Dad. When he was nervous or excited, he had a hard time finding his words too."

"Do I really? What else can you tell me about him?"

"Too much to say over the phone, young lady. Say, come on out for Sunday dinner. Then we can talk about Mike all you want. I'll even drag out the old albums. Know there's some pictures of your Dad in there."

"I'd like that, Jim. Thank you so much."

Sam was almost as eager as I was. Following Jim's directions, winding our way through the green hills, we were both silent. *Sam's probably just glad I finally found someone who can answer my questions and make his wife whole.*

"Hey, Jim must have invited family over too."

I had also noticed the cars parked around the well-kept house. I was disappointed that I would have to share my time with Jim. "I wish we'd made it some other day."

"I don't think he gave us much choice, honey. Sounded like a command performance to me." Sam grinned until I smiled back, knowing he was right.

Jim Woodbridge greeted us at the door. He was tall but no longer as slender as he would have undoubtedly been in his youth and his curly hair was so white one would never know what color it had once been. But his smile was welcoming. He shook Sam's hand, gave me a bear hug. "Come on out to the patio. Hope you like barbecue."

He led us down a short hall and through a cozy yellow and white kitchen to exit onto a cool, shaded patio, an area where several couples were gathered.

"I hope you don't mind but I called a few old buddies. They all have stories to share."

I could feel myself begin to choke on new emotions. "Mind? Oh, Jim, this is so kind...of all of you."

Food held little interest for me. I was filled up by the words swirling around me.

"We were a young, rather wild bunch. We needed his control. The Lieutenant was a great guy who knew when to be strict and when to act like one of us."

Pride swept through me.

"Yeah, Lt. Talbot didn't have to go out on that patrol.

He knew his men were worn out, hanging on by threads. So when the call comes from the CP to send out men to check on a suspected machine-gun nest in a nearby valley, he could have sent someone else."

"He led four guys. That valley was heavily mined, especially along the protection of the trees. They almost made it."

"Those damn mines were buried near the surface of the snow. Didn't take much weight to trigger them. Your Dad was out front."

Making an attempt to lighten the mood, another man, a Captain back then, laughed softly. "Mike could scrounge up the impossible better than any man I've ever seen. It was March, colder than a witch's . . ." he swallowed the words. "Well, ice cycles were forming inside the half-blown-up shack we'd set up as our CP. Mike found out it was my birthday. He rustled up and served champagne. There wasn't much, but it sure warmed us up."

"We very seldom slept in a foxhole. He'd run somebody out of their house or barn before he'd have his men dig a hole in that frozen ground."

I watched the men as they sipped beer and laughed, exchanging one story after the other. "Remember the time he gathered all those eggs so we wouldn't have to eat that powdered mess for breakfast?"

"He sure did enjoy life . . .and all the men around him. He laughed a lot, though there wasn't too much funny about those days. He talked about you and your mother too."

Barbecue never tasted so good. I had come here hoping for

one man's observations, but instead had been filled with enough word pictures to make the dreams of my Daddy come to life.

I was wearing a permanent smile when Sam put his arm around my waist and squeezed. "Feel better, honey?"

"I have my Daddy at last." I gave him a quick kiss. "Thanks for seeing me through this."

As we were preparing to leave, Jim handed me a flat tissue-wrapped package. "For some reason the Army missed this when they gathered up your Dad's belongings. I just packed it away with my memorabilia, not thinking too much about it until now. Funny about this," he said, touching the parcel. "Mike always had this with him, said it was his good luck charm. That night he left it behind on his bedroll."

With trembling hands, the taste of sweet closure in my mouth, I opened the tissue. The once-white background of the blocks was now a mellowed ecru, the bright blue triangles and pink squares faded to soft hues, but there was no mistaking the pattern. The "Cross and Crown" had come home.

~

.

ARKANSAS TRAVELER

Oh, hello, Ms. Marks. You've come for a teacher's home visit? I'm surprised that high school counselors still have the time. Oh, it's only for the seniors whose parents haven't been to Parents-Teachers Night? Well, I don't think mama will have time to sit down and talk now either. Jolene is comin' home.

Mama's cooked a big supper in anticipation. Those smells are delicious, aren't they? There's fresh string beans with tiny new potatoes seasoned with a chunk of salt pork simmering on the stove. Sweet potatoes candied in brown sugar and butter in that skillet on the back burner waitin' to be reheated. A nice pork roast is sizzlin' in the oven. See those yeast rolls risin' on the counter nearest the stove? They'll melt in your mouth. We'll have blueberry cobbler, and orange cake, and pecan pie to serve afterward with hot coffee to wash it down. Maybe you'd like to stay for a bite?

You can't? That's a shame, because mama is the best cook in the valley. Hands that come to work seasonally on the farm always come back because of her cookin', if for no other reason. When we have dinner on the grounds at church, folks gravitate to mama's fried chicken, black-eyed peas, and pumpkin pie.

Let's at least have a cup of coffee now. Would you like to try one of these fried apple pies? I make these all the time for our school lunches. You know I can't understand why mama thinks Jolene will appreciate all of her efforts. Jolene was the first child of six to graduate from high school, and she couldn't wait to get out of this mountain valley. The eldest boys went into the Army, and they stayed gone. None of them wanted anything to do with a rock-hard farm in the hills of Arkansas. Jolene was next in age, and she left just like the others.

I'm last, Ms. Marks, the youngest, twenty years younger than Jolene. I don't guess that I'll ever have the chance to leave. When I finish school, I'll find somethin' to do in town, and stay right here, I expect. I'm not like Jolene.

Jolene went to Little Rock first, to work as a secretary to an engineer in a computer company. Mama won't talk about it, pretends like she doesn't know anything, you know, but this engineer was a married man. With little ones at home. Pretty soon, Jolene's tellin' us that she's gettin' married and movin' to Dallas.

It's mighty hot in here. Shall we move to the porch?

The quilt? Oh, that's one I just finished. It is pretty, isn't it? The pattern is called Arkansas Traveler. Sort of looks like it could just keep movin' on, doesn't it? All them greens and golds and browns look like the trees and the leaves and fields you'd find all across the country, don't you think? I thought it would brighten up that wall over the fireplace. Who is she? Oh, that's a photograph of Jolene. You know one of those done in a studio where they place a white-feathered boa over your shoulders. Mama thinks it's right pretty. Myself, I've always found it too much for this plain, country-dressed room. It's gettin' faded with age, so I draped my quilt over the edge of the frame and spread it out for effect. You think I have the eye of a decorator? Well, I never thought about that, but I do like to make things pretty."

Oh, yes, we met Jolene's husband once. He was an older man, nice enough, I guess. He dressed in fancy western-cut slacks, soft blue shirt, and shiny cowboy boots-- wouldn't have lasted through one day in the fields as far as I could see. He laughed and joked with mama and daddy, showed lots of affection toward Jolene, and them drove off in that new midnight-blue Caddy, never to visit again.

Over the years, all we received were letters from her now and then, phone calls on special holidays once in awhile, photographs to chronicle her life. It must have been good. Big brick houses in a Dallas suburb, vacations in Europe, glossy pictures taken at fancy parties.

Would you like some more coffee, Ms. Marks? Another fried pie? What? No, Jolene never had a family. Said she'd had enough of large families. She wouldn't be tied down by no brats, she told me. She kept on workin' and travelin' and being photographed. To busy to be a mother, I guess.

No, she's comin' alone. Mama doesn't talk about it, of course, but I think her marriage is over. Why do I think that? Well, she's never come back here all these years, certainly never alone, now has she? She's gonna drive up with her tail between her legs, proclaimin' how sorry she is she neglected her poor old mama and daddy, wantin' to be soothed by mama, and makin' herself daddy's little girl once again.

Do you have to go? Well, lookie here, that cloud of dust must mean she's here. Maybe you'd like to wait and meet Jolene. Wouldn't you know she'd drive a red Mercedes. It'll be in pieces after a few months of drivin' up that road. See what I mean, Ms. Marks, isn't she beautiful? Look at that lime green dress billowing around her. Silk, wouldn't you guess? Watch her now...see, I told you she'd run up in tears and hug mama and daddy.

It's always been like this, Ms. Marks. I stand to the side while they laugh and cry and carry on somethin' awful when they hear from her. See, they never even introduced her to you, just walked right past us like we never lived. Jolene has come home and nothing else matters.

Ms. Marks, Ms. Marks, wait! I do thank you for being such a good counselor to me these past three years. I think I will take those college application forms you offered. Scholarship recommendations? That would be wonderful, Ms. Marks. Why have I changed my mind? Well, I need to look forward to my future, don't I? I'm thinkin' I can't stay here after all.

Why would I think that? Isn't it obvious?

Jolene is home.

~

KALEIDOSCOPE

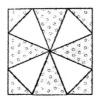

"How is she today, Maddie?" Cathie asked the nurse as she entered the special wing at Fairfield Care Center.

"She had one of her 'loud' days, Mrs. Shepherd." The black woman who cared for her mother chuckled as she locked the section door behind them. "I know she never learned those words at Bethal Baptist."

"Oh, no . . . " Cathie groaned. "She would be mortified if she knew. She hated it when Daddy let loose with that 'sailor talk' as she called it."

Cathie walked down the hall to the dorm-like room that her mother now called home. Standing along the wall were two patients, just standing . . . waiting. She was once again reminded of childhood days spent on the ranch, the way the cattle would do the same as these victims of Alzheimers–just stand around and wait. Cattle waited for the feed trough to be filled, but what were these poor souls expecting?

I don't want to remember her like this. Cathie stood watching the tiny figure rock, balanced on the edge of her bed. Her mother had become a stranger; forgetful, repetitive, at times downright belligerent. *How I hate this disease that's stolen mother and replaced her with a head full of nonsense on this frail body.*

She leaned over and kissed her mother's soft cheek. "Hi, Mama." The rocking stopped but she continued to stare out the window. "What's so interesting out there?"

She screeched at Cathie, "You haven't been here in months! You put me in this place with crazy people and left me."

"Mama, I was here yesterday. Remember? We had lunch together . . . your favorite, barbecued chicken."

A frown appeared across the translucent skin of her mother's face. When she looked up to meet Cathie's eyes, fear filled the faded blue eyes. "I. . . I don't remember. Oh, Cathie, am I going crazy?"

Cathie moved to the bed and, blinking back her own tears, gathered her tiny mother into her arms. "No, no, Mama. You're just tired, and you've been ill. It's hard to remember things when you're not feeling well. Tomorrow will be better."

Cathie stopped to speak to the nurse after her visit. "Does mother have any times when she seems more coherent? She seems so confused now, and angry."

The nurse paused for a moment and drew a deep breath. "She still knows enough to recognize that she's failing. It's a common phase of the disease, using hostility or fear. But she does have lucid days when she's around other people who are still able to talk about their travels, or when they show pictures and discuss their families. She even speaks up about her own history."

"Before Daddy died, they traveled the world. Most Navy career men would have been set on staying home. He said even if he had been there it was new, seen through mama's eyes."

"When her roommate started talking about her ancestor's arrival from Germany, your mother perked up. She didn't add much, but she seemed interested."

Cathie was encouraged and offered, "Her great grandparents crossed the country by covered wagon in 1846 to settle in Oregon. She's . . . she was quite proud of that."

"Maybe you could talk about some of those memories with her," Maddie suggested as she unlocked the door for Cathie.

The next day, lunch was a silent affair. Mama stared vacantly across the table. There was no response even when Cathie began to talk about her mother's pioneer family, the baby that died along the trail, the men who went on to build a lumber empire. *This isn't working.* Cathie tried not to let her frustration show as she tucked her mother's arm through hers. She noticed the elderly woman stooped more each day. Cathie wanted to cry out at the unfairness of the disease. She fought back fear that this was a scene she herself might recreate for her loved ones some day.

Settled back in the room, Cathie longed for her mother to be the way she was before. *Here sits the great cook who met me on Friday afternoon after school with a plate of hot cinnamon rolls, the playmate who learned to roller skate with me so I would have a companion when we lived on a remote outpost, the loving grandmother who had spoiled her only grandchild. And I want that person back.* But Cathie knew that woman was lost, gone.

"Mama, I went by your house today and picked up something special for you." She pulled the quilt out of the plastic bag and spread it across her mother's lap. "See the names embroidered in the circles? Who are they, Mama?"

The illusion of circular halos in the Kaleidoscope-patterned quilt was created by the use of light and dark fabrics. Its blues, pinks and many shades of floral done in octagon-shaped blocks in other areas, created rings of light seemingly throughout the whole creation.

Her mother listened as Cathie began to speak, pretending not to know much of the quilt's history. The empty gaze she often wore began to melt the sharp plans of her face. Her fingers slowly began to trace the circles and odd-shaped blocks.

Correcting her daughter, she said, "Oh, Cathie dear, you've got it all wrong. Your great-grandmother quilted this after reaching Oregon. She embroidered not only her family's names but also all of the ancestors she could remember. Then grandmother did her generation, and it passed on to my mother who did the same. It's become a memory quilt."

"Looks like a complete history of our family to me, Mama." Cathie squeezed her hand.

"You'll get it next, Cathie, and you must pass it on." Suddenly she was anxious. "But who will embroidery the names for this generation?" She began twisting her hands together.

Cathie hugged her close. "I will, Mama. You taught me all of the stitches, remember?"

A sweet smile broke across her mother's face. "Of course, you can, dear. That's the perfect solution." She clapped her hands together, the way Cathie had seen her do often when her Mother was delighted. She continued retelling the saga of the family, her eyes holding a sparkle Cathie hadn't seen in a long time.

This is how I'll remember Mama. The memories Mama is reciting are mine as well as hers. This quilt will speak for all of us from generation to generation, even if we no longer have the words.

~

IRISH CHAIN

I had certainly given those gossipy townspeople back in Plum Cove something to wag their tongues about. It was perfectly acceptable for me to purchase a train ticket to Chicago as I had often gone there before with father. It was quite another thing to book a sleeper from there all the way to Denver, one way, unaccompanied. I knew the ticket master to be a gossip of the first order, so I made sure that he received the news that I was going to be married. Of course, if those people peeking from behind their curtains at me knew that I had answered an ad for a mail-order bride, that would have set them on their ear. I could hear them now . . . that shameless Kate O'Brian.

"Denver! Next stop," the conductor called from the rear of the car. "Denver!"

At last, I thought. It had been a hard trip since we left St. Louis. As we had moved across the country, each stop meant further deterioration in the class of riders. This place called "the West" must be filled with all sorts of misfits if the passengers aboard this train were any indication. I was happy, in spite of the uncertainty ahead, to finally arrive.

Still, the thought of what faced me made my hands shake as I folded up the quilt I had somehow managed to finish this very morning with a flurry of lazy daisy stitches and double reverse chains.

"Is someone meeting you, miss?" The conductor asked as he helped me down onto the platform.

"I think so . . .I mean, yes, Mike Finnigan."

The man chuckled. "He's most likely forgot. He works that mine of his mighty long hours, I'm told. If he doesn't show up soon, ask the agent to get Ben Jenkins to carry you up to Silver Plume."

An hour later, I sat beside the grizzled team driver bumping along a well-worn road running up the mountain. The wagon, heavily loaded with an assortment of equipment, and sacks and barrels of supplies, slowly lumbered up the grade. Dust rose in a cloud, covering my dark green jacket and skirt with a sheet of gray particles. Even with a hat, and a handkerchief pressed against my mouth, I could feel and taste the dirt of Colorado through my entire being.

"Mike expecting you, Miss O'Brian?"

"Oh, yes. I sent him a telegram before I left Chicago so he'd know when I'd arrive."

"I guess he don't know then." He dug the yellow envelope out of his pocket. "Mike hasn't been into town for weeks. They sent this by me."

This fact only added more doubts about my venture on top of the pile that had been building since I left home. I could feel the knot in my stomach beginning to burn. Home? That had been wiped out with two blows; first, mother's death and then father's suicide last year...death before his embezzlement of bank funds was discovered. I resented the act that had caused my neighbors to consider me a criminal as well. Home? That would have to be created here in this wild country.

Silver Plume was made up of a small mercantile, several saloons, an unpainted church that at least had a steeple, Ma Barnes Boarding House, and a small bank with assay office attached. The jail was almost as large as the livery stable. Mike Finnigan's house stood in a grove of aspens near a stream on the hills overlooking the town.

It was an oversized shanty. The three rooms were smaller than the parlor in my old home. The furniture was crudely made, probably by the homeowner. There had been an attempt to make them appear more comfortable with some cushions on the rough settee, a pad on the benches drawn up before the potbellied stove standing in the center of the front room, and a pillow thrown on a nearby rocking chair. The bedroom was filled with more of the pine furniture; a bed with no coverlet, a chest holding what appeared to be a new pitcher and basin on one end with a wavy mirror hung over the other. Setting my valise down beside the trunk Ben Jenkins had placed at the foot of the bed, I sank down on the edge only to shudder at the sound of the corn husk filler in the mattress. My, what have I gotten myself into? I thought as I removed my hat and jacket. I wonder if Mike is as uncertain of this arrangement?

Entering the kitchen, I found the teamster waiting, hat in hand.

"Everything's unloaded, ma'am. I'll be heading back down. You know about lighting the kerosene lantern? Will you be okay if Mike's late?" At my nods to both, he continued, "Good. The pump brings water from the creek. Outhouse is back of the house near the barn."

When he was gone, I lowered myself into one of the chairs drawn up to the wooden table. Alone, I became once again caught up in my own anxieties. I reached out slowly and touched the metal plate still holding hardened food, wanting to make sure that this was real. I had been so convinced that my mind was made up, and that last letter from Mike Finnigan had decided my determination and future. Now that I was here, in this place to be called home, I began to question my sanity and tried to remember what he had written.

This is a beautiful country and I've found a vein of gold that is producing a comfortable living - enough for a wife and family. I'm a God-fearing man, no trouble with the law, never been married, and have no bad habits - unless you call a drink for special occasions, a love for this wild country, and some fiddle playin' now and then, as vices.

*I'll work hard at being the best husband I can be,
and treat you kindly. I know that this type of marryin' isn't
romantic, and that's important to womenfolk, but I am sure
from your letters that we will eventually form a mutual
attraction. Will look forward to your arrival.*

Very truly yours,

Michael (Mike) Dennis Finnigan

P.S. Silver Plume does have a church and a preacher.

I felt better remembering the letter. I took a deep
breath and stood. It was a new spring, a new year, and a new
life. I had to make this work. I just couldn't fail. There was
no place for me to go. This place could be made into a right
nice home. Men aren't good at keeping a place up, especially
when they work as hard as folks say Mike does. He had
purchased a new pitcher and basin. It had to be for my
benefit. And, after all, he had no idea when I would arrive,
or surely he wouldn't have left such a mess.

With the large, almost new wood stove, the well-
stocked shelves, and the pine table and chairs, the kitchen
wasn't really that bad. There was a window, uncovered for
the lovely view, with real glass. The room would look more
cheerful when I unpacked my trunk to add some bits and
pieces I had brought with me. I had a checked cloth that
would be just right for the table and. . .it was then that I
noticed the Mason jar filled with a collection of multicolored

wildflowers placed in the center of the table. The man who lived here enjoyed beauty.

Opening my valise and trunk, I began to add my own touches around the cabin. Doilies on the rough arms of the settee, scarves on the small tables and dresser top, a few colorful rag rugs scattered about each room began to brighten up the spaces. My books--histories, biographies, a few novels, and a dictionary-- were added to Mike's collections; mining tomes, many of the Classics, a book of poetry. The family Bible was placed on the top of the bookcase with a lacy scarf beneath it. In the bedroom I unpacked my personal belongings into empty drawers of the dresser. And, before I left the room, I spread the green-on-white Irish Chain-patterned quilt on the freshly-made bed.

The sun set and still no sign of Mike. Typing a large apron on, I began to go through the foodstuffs. In a short time I had a stew bubbling on the stove, pickled peaches in a bowl left from my mother's wedding set placed on the table, and rolls rising on the warming shelf above the stove. Mother's teapot and matching cups added a spot of color on the windowsill, the woven cloth adorned the pine top of the kitchen table and, with the added smells of good food, the room was indeed just as cheerful as I had envisioned.

I never heard him arrive. Suddenly, he was in the kitchen and the small room seemed to shrink even more. It wasn't only that he was tall, but he had such wide shoulders, and bulging muscles showing beneath rolled up sleeves of his denim shirt. With a head of curly black hair above a broad tanned forehead, and amused brown eyes surveying me from head to toe, I could only marvel at the fact that this nice looking man was to be my husband. As he looked me over, I wondered if I would do.

He finally spoke, with a voice that still held a touch of the Old Country. "If I had known you were to be here today, I would have met you at the train."

"The telegram didn't arrive in time, but . . . I know you would have been there." I struggled for the right words. "You've been busy."

"I hope that we never get too busy to . . . to not think about each other," he answered.

He will be able to care, I thought, almost dizzy with hope. We can build on that; respecting each other's feelings and thoughts and dreams.

I managed a smile. "Supper is almost ready."

He returned the smile, a wide grin that even touched his eyes. "Smells good. I'll just clean up."

As I fussed over getting the meal on the table, I found myself almost grinning with him. It was a good beginning.

Food dished up and rolls just coming out of the oven, I was pleased when Mike filled glasses with water, then pulled out a chair for me. He spoke as he sat in the place at the head of the table, "I like the touches you've added. New books to read, too. We can order more though the mail, you know."

I nodded in understanding. "I love the flowers on the table. I don't know the names of many of them."

"They're up in the mountains around us, in the high meadows." He smiled at me, a gentle touch in the look. "I'll show you."

Then, for a while, we were silent as we ate, both of us I'm sure wondering what needed to be said next. Mike spoke first.

"Are you a quilter?" I nodded before he continued. "The one on the bed is pretty. Does the design have a name?"

"It's called Irish Chain." I blushed. Had the pattern I had chosen long ago been an omen? "I find great joy in creating beauty with fabric and stitches and . . . " Across the table I met the dark gaze, halting my words, feeling as if I was babbling.

"Beauty is all around us, if we look for it." He grew solemn for a moment. Then he reached across the table to touch my hand. "It seems we're much alike, Kate. Do you think. . . I mean, I could talk to Parson Williams . . . that is, if you think we could make this work." He paused. "I don't think we'll change our minds, do you?"

I could feel a rosy flush rise up my neck and over my cheeks. "I'm sure we'll do just fine together, Michael Dennis Finnigan."

With a whoop, he was around the table and, swinging me up and off the floor and into his arms before I could protest. Warm lips covered mine as he spun me around. Deepening the kiss, Mike stopped moving, slowly letting my body slide down his until my feet once again found the floor. Whether from the spinning or the intimacy of the kiss, I was quite dizzy when he finally raised his head. It took a few minutes for me to catch my breath.

"Uh, Mike, I think we'd better see the Reverend first thing tomorrow."

~

BIRDS IN THE AIR

"But, Mama, yesterday you promised you'd buy some bread and peanut butter." Tyrone said, leaning over his mother's reclining figure on the worn sofa. "I'm hungry, Mama." Her breath smelled like rancid wine and the dull blue eyes she opened were bloodshot with puffy black circles beneath.

"Don't bother me, you hear. I done told you, I don't have any money." She put a shaking hand over her eyes. "I had to have some of my stuff. You know how my head aches if I don't get it." She rolled over, her back toward him. "Drink some Kool-Aid."

Tyrone knew better than to say any more. Mama would just get mad and yell and, if she was in "real need" of what he'd heard some of the older boys call the "Big H," he'd just get a smack up side his head or a vicious kick, neither of which she would remember later.

It was the same every month. The first week Tyrone could have eggs and bacon for breakfast and Big Mac's for supper; by mid-month he was eating dry TRIX out of the box and boiling his hot dogs. The last of the month he would seldom find anything in the cupboard or refrigerator . . .

nothing but those endless packages of drink and a handful of sugared flavors.

"I'll go see if Mr. Boudreaux's got some chores."

Often the old man in the tenement on Fourth Street would ask him to buy a paper for him or pick up his mail. In return, he'd offer Tyrone loose change or, what Tyrone liked even more, the old man would offer him a meal. Mr. B, as everyone called him, was from New Orleans. After all the years in New York, he still sounded funny when he talked but he sure remembered how to cook that Cajun food.

As he moved onto the stoop, a rusty sign hanging over the entrance squeaked in the stale breeze. He had always thought it was a dumb sign. Proclaiming the building as Green Street Plaza was just some joker making out like it was a fancy place overlooking Central Park or somethin'. If you had any view at all it was of either the tarred roof of other apartment buildings or the wall of broken windows in a building that hid the sky.

Up and down his street Tyrone saw young men "hanging out," heard the loud boom of radios blasting from all directions and noted the nasty words spray-painted on the walls. Burned out cars sat on the vacant lot along with shopping carts from a market blocks away. A rusty chain-link fence enclosed what was once a playground, concrete courts broken up with patches of weeds growing in the cracks, vandalized equipment no longer usable.

"What's happen', Tyrone?" Mr. Boudreaux greeted the boy when he opened the door. "Stayin' out of trouble?"

Tyrone wished the old man wouldn't remind him of the one time he had committed a little bit of a crime. "You know I am. That time you caught me with a loaf of bread was the first and only time I ever stole anything." He sat a saucer of milk down for the tiger cat pawing at his feet. "I was just hungry that day."

"That ain't no reason to steal." Mr. B had been quite rigid when making Tyrone return the bread and brought him to his home for a meal. "You 'bout ready for school?"

Mr. B sometimes thinks he's my daddy or something. "I'm not goin' to school."

"Whatcha mean?" Mr. B glared at the boy. "You're ten years old. The law says you have to go to school."

Tyrone sneered at him. "What law? You know those schools are crowded and dirty. No one cares if we learn or not."

"You should care. You're smart, son. Smarts can get you out of this ghetto."

"How, Mr. B? Am I gonna be given wings and fly out of here like a bird?" Tyrone laughed rather sarcastically, though something told him that Mr. B knew what he was talking about. Calvin and all those other boys hanging around on the street corners had dropped out of school and there was no where for them to go. But Tyrone wouldn't go back this fall. There was no money for clothes or supplies even if he changed his mind. He wasn't gonna have his classmates makin' fun of him.

Mr. B sent him off to gather the mail and buy a loaf of French bread to go with the gumbo simmering on the stove. When they had eaten, the old man, as usual, read to Tyrone while the boy washed the dishes. He had found a "space odyssey saga" in a thrift store and bought it to entertain him. Tyrone knew it was only make believe, those tales of settlements on far planets and the spaceship battles, but it didn't keep him from thinking how great it would be to fly high, away from these mean streets.

A fit of coughing brought the story to an end. Mr. B admitted he had been feeling poorly for a few days and asked Tyrone to pour him a tumbler of his "medicine" from the bottle kept next to the box of grits.

"Bring that quilt from my bed, Tyrone. I'll just wrap up and watch TV for a spell."

In the small back room Tyrone found the quilt neatly folded at the foot of the bed. When he spread it out to cover the old man's legs, he noticed the design of black figures on the yellow background.

"Sure is a pretty quilt, Mr. B."

"My granny made this quilt over a hundred years ago when she was still owned by Master John. See these black triangles and strips? They're made up to look like birds.

Granny called it the "Birds in Air" pattern. You know, when I lived over there on Waters Street an antique dealer stayed across the hall. He once offered me a hundred bucks for this here quilt."

"A hundred dollars." Tyrone's black eyes widened. "Wow!" He couldn't believe an old blanket would be worth that much.

"It would bring twice that much," Mr. B scoffed. "Wouldn't sell it for nothin' though." He chuckled. "May even be buried in it."

Promising to check up on his old friend the next day Tyrone hurried down the street toward his building. It was late. The slight figure in the growing dusk knew that after dark he'd probably hear gunfire, loud arguments, vicious fights. The cast of bad characters was already gathering; males shoving and pushing and bragging among themselves, pretend laughter from the women looking for a man who'd pay for their company.

When he reached the corner there was a dark Mercedes with tinted windows parked at the curb. He'd seen it often in the area. As he neared it, he saw the older boys, most of them wearing gold chains and expensive watches, saunter over in their new tennis shoes. The man, dressed in a silk suit and wearing dark glasses, spoke to them from the back seat. Just steps away from his own door and curious, Tyrone edged up to the group.

Calvin grabbed him by the neck of his T-shirt. "What you doin' here, Tyrone? Did yo cracker white mama send you?" The older boy laughed. "Let's see the green, little man."

"N-no one sent me." He tried to pull away but Calvin held on. "I was just lookin'."

"That nose'll get cut off, kid." Dark glasses spoke real smooth like. "You need a job?"

"W-what doin'?"

Calvin and the other boys hooted. "It ain't deliverin' flowers, Tyrone. You knows the score 'round here. Mr. Johnson here needs runners. Someone to take stuff to the sellers."

Tyrone shook his head. Mr. B had warned him about guys like these. Dealin' drugs would get him into more trouble than you could ever get out of, Mr. B always said. Tyrone didn't like what heroine did to Mama and he was sure he didn't want to try the stuff himself. So, in spite of the thought of quick cash, Tyrone backed away, then ran for the apartment door.

The stairs smelled of the stench of rotting garbage and urine. Only one bare light bulb hung high above them keeping each tread in shadows. Tyrone's steps echoed in the hollowness of the stairwell as he moved upward. He knew Mama would be gone. She always went out at night. . .often not coming home until dawn. Other times she brought men with her, men who didn't leave until the next day. All he could do now was slip inside, close the door, and bolt it against the outside ugliness.

It was well after midnight when Tyrone was awakened on his pullout couch bed by the sound of loud yelling accompanied by swearing. He heard the fumbling at the door right before recognizing Mama's giggles and the curses of the man with her. He scrambled up to slide the bolt.

"What took you so long, kid?" Calvin followed his mama into the room. *Why did Mama have to pick up one of those street kids to bring home with her? Was it because he reminded her of Daddy when he was young, a handsome black man she just couldn't resist?*

"I was asleep, Mama." He ignored Calvin. "It's awfully late, Mama."

"Since when are you my keeper, Tyrone?" His mama reached out and boxed his ears. "Get back to bed and mind your tongue around my gentlemen friends."

In the dark, Tyrone fought the tears. Once Mama had been a loving force in his life, someone who helped him with his homework, saw that he was dressed properly, made sure he ate well. Then she'd just given up. It wasn't long before she was hooked on drugs, marijuana first, then LSD. But it was heroin that became her master. In her lucid moments, and they were becoming fewer and fewer, she talked to him about how she had thought she could escape poverty, the bareness of her surroundings, by going into the nothing world of drugs . . .only to find that there was no getting away.

"I wasn't always fucked up, Baby." Tyrone hated it when she saw him only as a child. But he cried inside because most times she acted as if he was old enough to need no care.

It was noon before his mama shuffled into the living room, limp blonde hair covering her eyes, cigarette smoke causing her to cough. Tyrone wanted to remember how pretty she'd once been, how all the men in the neighborhood used to whistle when she walked up the street. It was different now. Men like Calvin had the money, or enough dope, to pay for time with his mama. But when she returned home alone, high, disheveled looking, those same men made fun of her, imitated her drugged walk as she made her way up the steps. Mama thought she had him fooled, that Tyrone didn't know what her life was all about. And he couldn't talk to her. But he had to go on trying to take care of her.

"Mama, do you have some money today? I could make you some toast if we had some bread."

"I gave you money yesterday, Tyrone."

"No, Mama, you didn't."

"Don't lie to me, boy!" She grabbed him. "What did you spend the money on? Something for that old man you visit?"

"Truly, Mama, you haven't given me any money for over a week." Tyrone protested.

"Are you callin' your mama a liar?" She screeched. "I just can't handle you anymore, Tyrone. You lie, you steal my money, and you always got that nose in my business." Her voice was getting louder, her eyes were blue spears stabbing at him. "Out! Get out of here! Don't you ever come back!"

"But, Mama . . . " Tyrone's heart was beating so loud he could hardly hear his own voice. "There's no place to go, Mama."

"Tough!" She hit him so hard he fell to the floor. "You're a little man now. With that smart mouth, you'll do just fine. Out!"

When she attempted to hit him again, Tyrone jumped to his feet, ran for the door and down the stairs. Sobs racked his body as he ran, dodging the evil of his neighborhood. When he reached Mr. B's apartment it took a long time for the old man to open the door. And he looked terrible! *Gee, he must really be sick. He needs me to stay here. I'll take care of him until he gets well. That'll be worth some food and a place to stay, wouldn't it?*

Mr. B didn't get better. For days Tyrone heated soup, placed cold towels on his forehead and kept the old man covered when racked with fever, he threw the quilt off. At the end of the third day the food was almost gone. He searched the drawers and cupboards but couldn't find any money. And Tyrone had to admit that Mr. B wasn't going to get well without help. He'd have to tell the apartment Super to call Social Services; Mr. B needed to go to City Hospital. But he was so old, he'd probably die. *Where will that leave me?*

When the Super went downstairs to call an ambulance, Tyrone returned to Mr. B's side. It was then that he noticed the quilt. That beautiful thing that, according to the old man, was worth a lot of money. Where he was going, he'd have no need for it. Someone at the hospital would cop on to it and that would be the end of the one thing that could help Tyrone out of this mess. He found a frayed wool blanket in the cupboard, reached down and replaced the quilt with it to cover Mr. B's trembling knees. Folding the piece up, Tyrone placed it in a garbage bag, leaving it near the front door.

Mr. B stirred when the paramedics lifted him onto the gurney. Thin hands fumbled around on the old blanket before they flung it aside to tuck him into heated sheets.

"Quilt? Where's my quilt?" The words were garbled with fever.

"What?"

"Took my quilt." His voice rose in a shaky shout.

"Know what he's talkin' about, boy?" One of the paramedics asked Tyrone.

"N-no, sir." The boy saw Mr. B's accusing eyes.

"Thief! Thief!" The old man hissed, pointing a bony finger at Tyrone.

"Settle down, pops." They strapped Mr. B down. "Know anything about a quilt?"

Tyrone gave the man a hard piece of a smile, then zipped up his jacket and moved to stand at the door. "Old man's been talkin' out of his head for days now."

As the gurney bumped down the stairs, Tyrone tucked the package under his arm, then closed the door behind him. He'd take the quilt to the antique stores down on Michigan Avenue. He knew he could sell it there. Not for a measly hundred bucks either. Tyrone vowed he wouldn't take a penny less than two hundred, but he'd ask for more up front.

If he had money, Tyrone could eat, find some place to sleep, take care of himself.

Or, as Calvin had told him, that kind of money would buy his start in the drug trade. He wouldn't need a job as a runner; he could make a pile of money all his own. Some other kid would be deliverin' packages from Mr. Johnson to him, Tyrone

Or maybe, just maybe, if he sold the quilt and took the money to Mama, she'd decide to let him come home.

~

.

HEAVEN'S PRAYERS

"Oh, God, he's not breathing! Call 911!"

For many months, each time I visited the grave, I heard those panic-stricken words echoing in my mind. I tried to believe there had been a purpose for Dylan's death but no matter how hard I thought, or how many times I prayed, the pain of losing him retained a heavy grip on my heart.

Dave never talked about his tiny son. Sometimes I could tell he hurt, could see it in his eyes when we happened upon a couple with a new baby or watched the shaky first steps of a niece. It distressed him to find me in tears so I bottled all the feeling inside when I was near him. It would have been better, I knew, if we'd talked it all out together. But we didn't.

Our closeness had also been shattered. We had been a couple since high school, friends before sweethearts. I would have never thought we would cease to lean on each other, hold each other in the darkness, love each other, no matter what happened. The few times during those first months when I had reached out to touch Dave in the dark or pressed close to him as I welcomed him home, he had quickly pulled away. After a few attempts, I had become just as remote.

I spent a lot of my free time with my mother. Her warmth and the comfortable surroundings of my childhood home offered a welcome refuge.

"I think you should join a support group, Emma." Mother suggested one morning while placing a hot cup of tea before me. "Men are different. They don't seem to be able to talk about their pain and loss. We women, on the other hand, find solace in sharing, talking out our fears and heartache."

"I don't know, Mom." I wasn't sure I could bare my soul about the crib death of my first child, especially with a bunch of strangers.

"You need to talk to other mother's who've been through this, honey."

It took months for me to make the decision.

Later, as I strolled toward my rendezvous with Dylan, I was drawn to a small headstone with sculpted lambs around the edges. Kneeling down, I read the inscription:

CONNOR J. KENNEDY: Born May 31. Died June 1, 1998. "You only stayed for a little while but you will always be in my heart."

Those words chiseled in stone spoke of my feelings so eloquently and offered so much comfort that I often found myself walking across the grass to gently touch the stone when I visited the cemetery. No one but another mother could have chose those words and my heart reached out to her wherever she was. *Please, dear Lord, fill her with hour comfort and give us both the strength to go on.*

During the Christmas season a small-decorated tree appeared on Connor's grave, then there were weeks with nothing. It concerned me that it was seldom visited so I decided to add special touches to both babies' places. Somehow tending the graves eased some of the pain I still felt. And maybe this caring was what led me to join a support group.

One afternoon I stroked my son's headstone. "Dylan . . . I've decided to go to this meeting and – well, try to talk about you and your . . . death, how much you meant to me. Maybe, if I can help myself, I can get your daddy to talk about you, too."

At the meeting's, others who had experienced the premature death of a child surrounded me. During the first few sessions I listened to their stories, shared their tears. These people understood. The next step, telling them about my baby, was almost easy.

"My son, Dylan, was born almost on the day he was due." I could feel my throat tighten up but pressed on. "He was such a fat, perfect baby, it's so hard to. . . I mean no one saw that he had underdeveloped lungs, no one told us he should be closely watched." I took a deep breath. "He moved . . . turned his head into the bumper pad. I've always wandered if . . . if I hadn't placed him near the side of the bed . . ." I broke off, tears strangling off the words.

"You mustn't blame yourself, Emma."

"I think Dave blames me." I blurted out.

"It's not anyone's fault, honey."

"No one really knows what causes this, Emma."

"God had a purpose for it, dear."

I rejected the idea that God had planned this. How could He take away a baby, a child needed by his mother and father, with no explanation? No reason? I just couldn't understand.

Certainly Dave wouldn't accept this God bit. He refused to discuss the support group or anything else about the death of his son. Would he blame me forever? Did Dave think we could on like this day after day, never acknowledging a child we had both so desperately wanted, loved from the first moment and lost too soon? What . . . no, *where* was our future?

One afternoon I went to the cemetery with sewing bag in hand. The day before I had placed fresh flowers in the small urn and pulled weeds missed by the caretaker. It was peaceful, a soothing atmosphere to sew in. I often sat there with Dylan, whispering comforting words, pretending . . . oh, I don't know what I expected, but I looked forward to the visits.

Removing the wooded hoop from the bag, I began to stitch through the three layers, quilting the pieces together. I had been quilting since my grandmother gave me basic lessons at age twelve. Dave had often teased, telling anyone who would listen that I paid more attention to my sewing than his high-school football performance. But it was he who purchased the Hawaiian quilt pattern book on our honeymoon and insisted I had to have the colorful island fabric for a backing, fabric that I had placed in the bottom of the cedar chest to await a special project. And now I had chosen one.

When I told Dave I was surprised, then hurt, at the angry words the idea produced.

"How can you even think of celebrating a death?"

His words were like a knife piercing my soul. I wanted to turn away, forget my plans, appease him. I stopped. It was time to face this thing . . . this silence, then anger. Right now, here today. The only option I had was to stand my ground, make peace with our son's death and move on, even if it meant going it alone.

"It'll be a year on June 1 since Dylan's birth. I'm making this banner for his grave." I picked up the wrought-iron frame with prongs to push into the soil. "Actually, I'm making two of them. There's another grave. Another baby someone lost a year before ours. It's not visited often so I've been caring for it, too. The second banner is for Connor."

I can't believe you're doing this." Dave's eyes filled with anguish, his face took on an angry flush. No matter how his words wounded, Dave was finally talking. "Doesn't it tear you apart to go there? To know you'll never hold him, see him walk, or . . ." His voice broke.

I sucked in a painful breath. "It comforts me to go there. I feel close to Dylan." I saw the look of surprise. "Won't you come with me, Dave?"

He looked stunned that I would even ask. "I . . . I can't. He's dead, Emma! Don't you realize . . . how can you pretend to talk to him! That's crazy. Our baby's gone and you . . ." He turned away, standing erect, gazing out the window.

"You think it was my fault."

"W-what?" He turned back to me, frowning. "What did you say?"

"I've always had the impression that you blame me for Dylan's death. That you felt I was careless when I put him to bed." My voice began to shake. "That I was responsible for him suffocating."

"No, no, oh, God, I never meant for you to feel that way." A confusion of emotion played across Dave's face. Then I watched it crumble as he reached out, pulling me fiercely into his arms, tears flowing. The words tumbled over each other as he began to speak. "You were so distraught, I felt that I had to stay strong for you. I was afraid to speak his name. I knew if I opened up, I'd fall apart. Then you'd be all alone . . .we'd both be lost."

I snuggled closer to his warmth. "A man's not supposed to grieve, to cry?"

"Dad always said tears were a sign of weakness." The pain was out in the open now; I could see it, realize that it had been there all along. *Had I been too afraid to deal with his loss, too?*

"I never knew you could love someone instantly," Dave continued, "but the moment he was placed in my arms, I was overwhelmed." His voice shook. "Why did we have to lose him. Why?" His shoulders shook with sobs.

I cradled him in my arms. "Sh-sh, honey, it's going to be all right. People in my support group assure me we'll get past the deepest of this pain. When you talk about it, Dave . . .when you share your grief with others who've been through the same loss you feel such relief."

Dave wiped his eyes on a shirtsleeve. "I'm sorry, honey. I turned away from you when you needed me most."

"I thought you no longer loved me."

He drew me closer. "I've always loved you, Emma. I . . . I was scared, too, afraid that if . . . if we had another child, it might die. I couldn't imagine us surviving that again."

*   *   *

On the first day of June Dave accompanied me to the cemetery. We decorated Dylan's grave with a ceramic Teddy bear laying on it's back holding red roses in his belly, colorful balloons tied to a paw. The banner holder went easily into the soft ground. Slipping the quilted piece, white background with blue pattern appliquéd on top backed by the colorful Hawaiian print into the frame, it seemed to blossom under the bluest of skies and the warmest of sunshine above the tiny grave.

"Happy Birthday, Dylan." Dave kissed the stone, put an arm around my shoulders and we moved down the path.

"Hello, Connor." He patted the stone lightly before erecting the second banner.

We stood looking at the banner before us, noting that we could also see our son's place several rows away. They were perfect pieces of art. I had chosen this particular Hawaiian print not only for its beauty but also for the meaning. "Heavens Prayers," it was said, had been first created when the quilt maker was going through a personal tragedy. The center of the design depicted hands reaching out in prayer to the four corners of the earth. The starflower in each corner, with holes cut in the middle, indicated the gateway to the spiritual world.

A soft voice behind us said, "I must thank you."

A young woman, blonde hair flowing, slender figure clad in jeans and dark T-shirt, moved to the opposite side of the grave, bending down to place a small bouquet of daisies on the grassy mound. Rising, she offered her hands, one to each of us. "I'm Connor's mother, Julie Kennedy."

"I'm Emma." I nodded at my husband. "Dave. We're . . . we're the parents of Dylan . . ." I pointed. "Over there."

"You've put other things here." Her soft brown eyes caught mine. *Was she upset with me? Oh, Lord, You know I had never meant to condemn her absence.*

"Yes . . . yes, I have. I never saw anyone here . . ." I was making this worse. "I wanted to tell you how comforting your words were, the inscription spoke to me. When I visit . . . my son, I stop to see Connor, too."

"Thank you so much." Tears filled her eyes. "Soon after . . .after Connor died, my husband was transferred, and we moved out of state. I haven't been able to visit the cemetery very often. I prayed for you, you know."

I looked at her, confused. "But we've never met."

"I prayed for someone – you know, sort of a surrogate woman – to take care of Connor for me. I know God sent you."

~

SHOO FLY

"Thee should remember we do not approve of school past the eighth grade. Against my best judgment, I allowed thee to continue. Now, this talk of college. Thee knows the answer to that." Daat didn't raise his voice answering Rachel's request, but his blue eyes flashed a warning. "Thee should be learning the household duties. Have thee yet begun to work on the bridal linens?"

Evening meals were not silent as the noon one was; every family member was allowed to join in discussions, question their elders, and voice an opinion. This gave Rachel's brothers an opportunity to poke fun at their younger sister.

"She makes only quilts - lots of quilts." Benjamin teased. "To keep her warm because she has no husband."

Micah laughed. "Why should she work on bridal linens when no one is seeking her for marriage? She's seventeen, an old maid already. Men want young brides."

"She'd rather be in the barn with the cows and horses," Levi added.

It was true, every word of it, Rachel thought, as she felt her face begin to burn from the blush creeping upward. I should have been asked for long ago. It's true that my chest should be filled with embroidered bed and table linens; instead mine holds only quilts, lots of them. I should have been born a boy, she mused. With my love of animals, I would have made a good farmer. And maybe if I had been male, I would not have this longing for more education either.

She knew Samuel was watching her. She could feel his eyes. She wouldn't look up. She didn't want to see the question, and know she must pretend to not understand. Now, when she had prayed so hard that Daat would understand and change his mind about her schooling, and

he had decided to stick to the old beliefs, Rachel knew Samuel would ask her that special question again. She couldn't think about a different answer from the "no" she had given earlier, even though her dearest hopes and plans had been crushed.

"Samuel, are thee still planning to leave on Saturday? Are thee sure thee won't stay longer? There is more we can teach thee." Daat asked the young man on his left.

Although Rachel was waiting for his answer, the sound of the strong, well-cultured voice filled the room, and caused her to quiver inside.

"It's time, Mr. Yoder. I'm grateful for your sharing of knowledge, but I must be going home."

Samuel Kurtz would have been welcome to extend his apprenticeship in furniture making as long as he felt necessary. He had come to them highly recommended, and had more than earned his place with the work he had put out while being tutored. But he had spent many months here and it was now time to go on with his plans to open his own shop back in Ohio. He also knew he must leave this farm before her father knew the fact that he had fallen in love with Rachel.

Rachel had known how he felt even before he spoke to her. She had felt something within herself answer those glances he had offered across the table. And it made her afraid though she didn't quite know of what. But she no longer smiled at him across the table, or allowed him to touch her when they were alone in the barn. When he had proposed, she had given him her answer, even though she longed for all he had offered her.

"I do love you, Rachel," Samuel had told her. "I'm not asking you to give up everything. There isn't that much difference between the Mennonites and Amish sects."

She had managed to laugh. "Oh, ye think not? Thee doesn't dress plain." Rachel poked a finger at the blue and white-stripped shirt he wore. "Thee has a nice car, and thee loves radio music."

"Need I point out that I heard you singing along with Reba one morning as you hooked up the milkers?" He grinned at her, dark eyes speaking a language she was just learning. "It's rather silly to allow electricity in the barn, but still have kerosene lanterns and wood stoves in the house."

"The District Church elders believe such modern devices interfere with family life," Rachel had explained, then put up her hand warding off further words. "Let's not argue religion, Samuel."

"Don't you want to marry someone you love instead of a man your father chooses?" He had placed his hands on both sides of her face, and leaned down to kiss her, not for the first time, but more tenderly than before. "I know you care for me, Rachel. Please marry me."

Her blue eyes filled with tears. "I. . .I am fond of thee, Samuel, but thee asks too much. Daat would shun me if I don't marry one of my own. I am my mother's only daughter. She. . . she would be all alone here." Rachel brushed the tears off her cheeks. "Though thee are a good man, Samuel Kurtz, thee are still considered an outsider."

"Ah, yes, an Englisher, as you would say." Then Samuel used the most important dream she had shared with him. "What about the teaching certificate you want? Your father won't agree when no other girl in Lancaster County has ever been allowed to attend college. Yes, Rachel, he is a good man, but he can't see any future for you except the one that he will impose."

She had twisted shaking hands together, and lowered her head, unwilling to see the pain in his eyes. "He is my Daat, Samuel. I cannot go against his wishes."

"He'll have you married within the year." Samuel spit out the words. "And by the time you would have graduated from college, you'll have two or three babies."

"Thee doesn't like children?" The surprise showed in Rachel's voice.

"Of course, I do. I'd want a family with you, Rachel. After you finish college and begin teaching."

Her thoughts had been so scrambled. "Thee would want me to teach?" Before she heard his answer, her mind was running ahead. Maybe Daat would allow her to go on to school, if he knew that she could have a career and marriage.

"It's your dream, Rachel. I want you to be happy."

On that day she had been so sure that her dreams would come true. It had sounded so wonderful. Samuel was very special. What a good husband he could be. He loved her enough to allow her to teach, be married to him, and have a family. She felt sure Daat could be swayed just once again; after all, he had allowed her to continue through high school. Surely he could see that she would make a good teacher.

And now she had received his answer.

Rachel helped her mother clear away the dishes. Then, excusing herself, she fled to her room. Tears of disappointment slipped out as she pulled the small frame down from the ceiling. Brushing them away, she sat down and continued the tiny stitches through the burgundy and pink pattern of her latest quilt. Rachel had chosen the "Shoo Fly" pattern with it's repeated blocks of squares and triangles accented with small purple diamonds, because of Samuel's love for her Shoo Fly pie. Tasting heavily of its molasses base and topped with crumbs, Shoo Fly pie was the simplest of pies to make, but he raved about it. She began the quilt, not thinking until it was almost completed that it would make a beautiful addition to a newlywed's home. Her creation would now be a parting gift.

It was well past midnight when Rachel completed the stitches, rolled the piece up, and placed it on the chair for delivery to Samuel. Turmoil continued to grip her as she changed into the flannel nightgown and brushed out the strawberry-blonde hair that had never been cut. Had it been sinful that one time to let her hair down, and for Samuel to run his fingers through the silky strands? It had been such a tender gesture. . . was she never to know such a touch again?

She didn't sleep well and was almost late for the morning milking. It was her task to hook up the electric milkers, then to empty the milk into large stainless-steel cans for pickup by the processor's tankers, and to clean the equipment in preparation for the evening milking. She hurried through the hooking up, then turned to shovel grain into the troughs.

Later, Rachel knew when Samuel entered the barn. Her hands began to shake as she unfastened the cups from the cows. Silently, they worked side by side until all the machines were pulled up and out of the way, the containers emptied and moved into the washing area.

"I'm leaving tonight, Rachel. I'll stay overnight at the hotel in town." Samuel placed his hand over hers. "I won't make it hard on you by repeating my proposal, but I want you to know that I'll carry love for you with me. All I spoke of before can still be yours." He rose, walking to the door, then turned to add, "I'll wait for you tomorrow until nine."

The remainder of the day was a blur. After the main meal, Rachel sat in the kitchen peeling apples while her mother rolled out dough for pies to be taken to the barn raising on Saturday. It would be a day to visit with other families as everyone turned out to help.

It was hard to look at Samuel sitting across the table at the late meal. Something urged her to memorize the way the dark hair fell across his forehead, see once more the smile that made his face light up, and file away the sound of the laugh he gave to one of Micah's comments. But when he met her gaze, there was no happiness in it, no laugh lines around the mouth that had kissed her so sweetly.

"We're sorry to see thee leave, Samuel." Mother patted his shoulder as she sat down a large pan of bread pudding before him.

"I'll miss all of you, Mrs. Yoder." Sad eyes caught Rachel's. "You've not only given me a wealth of knowledge about the furniture making, but treated me like a member of your family. I very much appreciate that."

Rachel thought she would choke on the feelings floating between the two of them. She pushed the food around on her plate, hoping to finish the evening without anyone realizing just how upset she was. When Samuel had drawn the meal out as long as he dared, he excused himself to begin loading the car with his belongings. Rachel hurried upstairs, picked up the quilt, and slipped into his room to leave it with the rest of his belongings. Then she eased back into her room, closed the door, and leaned against it, taking deep breaths to ease her racing heart.

On his last trip to the car, Samuel paused outside her door, and spoke softly, "Thanks for the gift, Rachel." He waited for a moment. When she didn't answer, he went back down the stairs, and she listened to him leave, tires crunching on the graveled drive.

Burying her face in a pillow, Rachel sobbed. Why does it hurt so much? Can you truly fall in love forever with a man you have not known all of your life? Am I a coward to not consider leaving my family to join the outside world? Would Daat actually shun me if I accepted Samuel's proposal? Couldn't he forgive me for wanting to marry someone I love, and for also yearning for a career?

"Rachel?" her mother called out before entering the darkened room. Sitting on the edge of the bed, she placed an arm around her daughter's shoulder. "Thee is crying over Samuel."

It was a statement that required no affirmation. Her mother continued, "Samuel has spoken to me." She overlooked her daughter's gasp of surprise. "Do thee love this man, Rachel?"

Fresh tears flooded Rachel's eyes. She nodded. "But Daat would not understand."

"It's not Daat's happiness that I am concerned about." She rose to light the lamp, the light throwing out a rosy glow in the room. She smiled as she noted her daughter stiffen, stunned. "Thee are my only daughter and I want happiness for thee. Rachel, thee has always been different. . .smart, but dreamy, wanting things beyond our way of life."

"I want to be a teacher, Maam."

Samuel says he will see that thee goes to college after you are married. Do you want to marry him, Rachel?"

Rachel didn't know if she had the words her mother wanted to hear. "I love him, Maam. I want to be with him, build a life with him, have his children."

"Then I will speak to Daat." She rose. "He was going to talk with thee in the morning about marriage to Aaron Beaman."

"But I hardly know Aaron!" Rachel almost wailed.

Her mother patted her hand. "I know, Rachel, but Daat thought it would be a good match for thee. I will make him understand where your heart is."

"W. . .will Daat shun me, keep thee from seeing me?"

Her mother sighed. "I do not know, my daughter." She moved to the door. "Pack thee belongings. Micah can take thee to the hotel in the morning. Thy chest and furniture will be sent later."

Unable to sleep with the wonder of it all, at dawn Rachel was in the barn doing her usual chores. Her emotions were jumping up and down. One moment she could hardly wait to see Samuel, then the next she feared what Daat would say to her mother. Can I go through with it if he forbids me to ever see maam again? As she returned to the house, Rachel met Daat on the back porch where he was washing up for breakfast. She would have to wait no longer for her answers.

"Has thee shamed us with Samuel, Rachel?"

She felt her face flush. "Of course not!" When she heard how sharp she sounded, Rachel felt she must admit to some improprieties. "I. . . we have held hands." She met the probing blue eyes. "And. . .I kissed him."

Daat shook his head. " I can believe thee would have to experiment, daughter. I do not wish to know what happens to you when you go out into the world." Did that mean he would shun her? Or give her his blessing?

He spoke to her brothers about work for the day, and ignored Rachel throughout the entire meal. Rachel caught her mother's eye, but she gave no indication of what had happened between the two adults. As she cleared the table, Daat directed his instructions to Micah.

"Thee will hitch up the buggy and take thy sister to the hotel."

Micah's eyes widened for a moment, then he smiled gently at Rachel. She stood still, in shocked silence, waiting for Daat to speak to her.

"I will not speak to thee after today, Rachel, for thee has broken with our life." Daat would not meet her eyes. "Maam, I will not forbid thee contact with her as it would bring thee much sorrow." Then he left the room without a backward glance.

"Send me thy address when settled," Maam reminded Rachel as she hugged her close. "I am glad that thee has a choice for your life. I was very unhappy for a long time after marrying Daat. I wanted to be something more than a wife and mother. It has worked out for me, but I wanted more freedom for thee."

In the hotel lobby, Rachel sat waiting for Micah to find Samuel. Dressed in her prettiest purple dress, she hoped that she would please him. She removed the white Amish cap. Pulling the pins from the bun, she let her hair down to frame her face, and fall down her back. It would have to do until she could find some way to contain it. The new look brought a welcoming smile from Samuel as he followed Micah down the stairs.

Micah hugged her, then placed her hand in Samuel's. "Take care of her, Samuel."

"Forever, Micah, forever."

Samuel rushed out to tuck her into his car, the first one she had ever been inside. He sat there for a moment, then pulled her into his arms. "I'll have to put you up with my sister until we can post the bans at the church. That will give us some time to find a place to live, and set it up. And your beautiful quilt will cover us when we make love every night."

"Samuel!" Rachel looked into the love mirrored in his eyes. "Every night? Oh, my."

He laughed loudly, the lost happiness returned. "I do love thee, Rachel Yoder." And the kiss they exchanged went a long way toward proving just that.

Then Samuel started the engine and drove them through the harvested fields, past the centuries old stone houses, and straight out of Lancaster County into a new life.

~

OREGON FLOWERS

"You need meat, Kate. You've got to regain your strength and be able to nurse little Davey." Dave, placing his sweat-stained hat on, and picking up his rifle, was ready to move out.

"I don't want you to go, Dave. Those signs of Indians you saw yesterday were. . . "

He stopped her with a quick kiss. "They won't bother with a lone wagon, honey. Now, you have plenty of water and shade here. Work on your quilt. You never get enough time for that. I'll be back before dark."

Kate held the two-week old baby close as she watched her husband walk across the prairie until he faded into the horizon. She couldn't have stopped him. Dave would always do what he thought best, no matter what she wanted. Just as he had sold a prosperous farm, bought this prairie schooner and set out for Oregon, paying no mind to her fear of giving birth on the trail.

"Don't worry, Little Davey." Kate kissed the soft cheek of her son before placing him back in the basket. "Now, let's get these chores done." She shook out and refolded the linens they had used sleeping outside of the wagon. It had been too hot under the canvas top so they bedded down beneath the stars. Dave thought all of this was such an adventure. Couldn't he see how afraid she was, leaving her home, doing all of this?

She drew water from the river and placed it on the fire. When it reached a boil, she threw in handfuls of dried beans. If Dave found no game, they would still have to eat. Adding biscuits and coffee wouldn't help the monotonous meal much, but it was all she could do. At noon, Kate ate some dried apples pieces with a cup of tea, glancing across the prairie, hoping to see Dave's returning figure. When Little Davey began fussing, she climbed up into the wagon and nursed him, continuing to search the waves of grass with eyes the color of the endless sky.

"He'll be back soon, Little Davey. Your father's itchin' foot probably carried him farther than he planned."

The baby slept while Kate set needle to the quilting of her latest piece. She had started the Oregon Flower pattern at home on her quilting frame, just one of the precious things she wanted to move with her but had to leave behind. She had picked the broadcloth and chintz materials from Mr. Barnes' Mercantile, cut and sewed the blocks by lamplight at night while Dave mended harnesses or sharpened the ax. The muslin backing with the inside cotton pad had just been stitched to the blocks when Dave walked in to say he'd found a buyer for the farm so they could head West.

Kate shook herself free of the memories, turned bitter now by the hardships of the trail. She pushed the needle in and out of the layers of cloth, creating swirls of neat stitches over the light pieces, and feather stitches done in soft pinks and greens on the white background. Darkening shadows accompanied the finishing stitches, driving her outside. Standing still for a moment, staring off in the direction Dave had gone, Kate felt her heart begin to pound heavily against her ribs. Where was he? He should have been back long ago. It occurred to her for the first time that he might not come back.

She fed Little Davey again and then tucked him into a box inside the wagon. Pulling out the extra carbine, Kate made sure it was loaded before she picked up the basket to begin collecting dried chips and what dead wood she could find. She'd have to keep a fire going through the night, if for nothing more than her feeling that the light could provide a beacon. Later, she ate some of the beans and biscuit, sipping a cup of coffee before feeding the fire and climbing back into the wagon. Sleeping outside was no adventure when you were alone. She leaned back against the inside of the wagon, trying to stay awake.

She dozed. When she opened her eyes again, Kate could hear the restless horses, whinnies rising. Probably just flies, she thought as she settled down again. When she next opened her eyes fully, the moon was just coming up. Feeling chilled, she pulled the quilt around her shoulders. The horses were still moving around. Maybe they needed water.

Kate was stepping off the wheel when she heard the muffled sound of hooves. When she turned, looking for the source, two horses moved into the dim light of the dying campfire. She pressed her back against the wheel, watching the horsemen as they watched her. Their hair hung in two stiff braids to their shoulders; they were naked to the waist. One of them held ropes on her horses, the other dismounted and walked toward Kate. He held a knife in one hand. In the other was Dave's rifle.

Kate knew when she saw it. Bile rose up into her throat. Dave was dead. A shiver grabbed her as the pain of her loss rolled over her. Had it been quick? Or did these savages torture him as she had heard about in St. Joe? Was she to be next?

There was a terrible odor to the man as he drew near. Kate noticed the shiny hair and guessed that what she smelled was some kind of animal fat. The nauseous feeling almost overtook the cold fear she felt as he reached out.

The dirty hand never touched her. Instead, it softly stroked the quilt around Kate's shoulders. She tried to pull back. In guttural noises she could not understand, the Indian began shouting. Then he suddenly tugged on the quilt. Kate clutched it even tighter. He raised the hand with the knife. Kate waited for the blow, then quickly released the cloth, suddenly remembering the responsibility she had sleeping soundly in the wagon.

"He like pretty blanket." The mounted Indian spoke.

"T-take it. . ." Her voice shook when she answered. "It's. . . it's a gift."

The mounted Indian spoke in the same unrecognizable sounds. Kate watched in fascination as the other man handed Dave's rifle to the speaker, sheathed the knife, and wrapped himself up in her quilt. He mounted his horse, then moved it to Kate's side. He leaned over and handed her the woven ropes securing her horses. His glittering black eyes caught hers. "Gift."

Then the pair wheeled their horses about, and rode off into the shadows.

Kate built up the fire, then scrambled back up to the now whimpering Davey. Still shaking, she cried, whether for Dave or herself she wasn't certain. It was a long time before she calmed.

At dawn, Kate broke camp, hitched the horses to the wagon, and climbed up on the high seat. Leaning the rifle against her leg, with Davey snuggled in the basket placed beneath the seat, Kate clicked at the horses after she released the break.

"Off we go, Davey. It couldn't be so hard to get to Oregon. Your father said it was only a few hundred more miles. We'll just follow the river."

~

FLOWER GARDEN

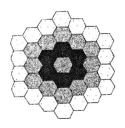

When I get really upset, I clean house. The night Jerry told me he was leaving me for Trish Taylor, I started with the mold in the grout of the shower tiles. By the time he had packed his bags and loaded his golf clubs and collection of Ellery Queen mysteries into his new pickup, I had started on scrubbing the baseboards.

By three a.m. I had cleaned out all of the kitchen cabinets and moved into the guestroom. No way was I going to sleep in that familiar king-size bed facing a mirror that had often shown the two of us in an embrace. All I would ever be able to see now would be Jerry snuggled up with that bleached-blonde bimbo from his office.

I both hated and craved the concern I received from my best friend, Sandy. Then she asked the million-dollar question. "What ever are you going to do? I mean . . .you have to eat and everything."

As I sat across from her, still dressed in a bathrobe at noon, it did dawn on me that I was going to have to get my act together, find something to do with the rest of my life. Yesterday I would have been beginning my usual daily routine. . .keeping house, cooking dishes Jerry loved, working on my latest quilt. Now I faced the reality of what life really looked like. I had been dumped. I was going to be a divorcee. I was going to be alone. Oh, my God, how can I live with it all? The embarrassment, the lack of money? The murmurs were still resounding in my head when it hit me that this so-called great marriage hadn't been so wonderful. But it was the only one I had. And that made it hard to let go.

"I'll think of something, Sandy. Sure it hit me hard. You know why? I found out that my quiet, supposedly hardworking husband had been warming the bed of a former Pineville High School cheerleader for over a year . . ." I paused, letting the words sink in. "And I was too dumb to know it." The realization of what a fool I had been made it easier to start divorce proceedings.

"Okay, so he's a jerk. That doesn't answer my question. What can you do to make a living? You married right out of school . . ." Sandy stopped, her mouth falling open. "You wouldn't think of going back to carhopping'?"

"Since every drive-in ten counties has been closed for twenty years, I seriously doubt it." I gathered up my shoulder bag and jacket. "I can waitress though."

"Kelly Anderson, you'll be the laughing stock of Pineville."

"You do whatcha gotta do, honey." I laughed at the look on her face. Sandy did not want to be the best friend of a common waitress. "I don't know what work I will do but I do know that I'm going to work off this flab. Then I'll buy a new wardrobe, go dancin' at Billy Bob's and never give spit for another man."

Of course, it didn't work out that way. I did join the Diet Bar where the counselors put me on a regimen of weightlifting, treadmill jogging and aerobics, plus a low-fat, almost vegetarian diet. That first day, after all the huffin' and puffin', with the soreness already setting in and faced with that 900-calorie menu, I went home to eat all the snacks in the house. Well, I couldn't afford to throw them out, now could I?

And I guess word got out that I was thinking of seeking employment at one of our many esteemed eateries. You know, places like Burger Barn or Harry's Grill. I never made it to apply. Merrilou Campbell approached me when I returned my latest stack of art books to the county library.

"I hear you need a job. I'm looking for a library clerk. It'll pay less money than salary plus tips at Harry's but you won't get your butt pinched here," she pointed out.

I spent my mornings checking in and shelving books, my lunch hour doing aerobics after a couple of carrot sticks and a power bar. Afternoons I assisted patrons while Merrilou did whatever head librarians did in their offices behind closed doors. Before heading home for a frozen diet dinner, it was back to the Diet Bar to pump iron and run a few more miles on the treadmill.

Coming to the conclusion that I had to make a clean break with the past, I rented a bright, airy place in an old cotton warehouse that developers had renovated into apartments. It had quickly become home with its open plan, lovely wooden floors, exposed brick walls, windows that went on forever and room for my quilting frame. I decorated the walls with quilt pieces I had packed away, never knowing what I would do with them. They made a beautiful addition to this place I could now truly call home. As soon as the house sold, per the stipulation of the divorce court, I was seriously thinking about putting a down payment on the apartment.

Nights when I couldn't sleep and those long weekends after shopping for rabbit food and completing my exercises, I would sit at the frame and work on my creations. The frame now held my latest piece, a large quilt to cover my new bed. The pattern was called "Flower Garden", a landscape of mauve and lavender flower centers on a pale pink background. I was just beginning the tiny stitches done by hand to attach the blocks through the batting to the solid green backing.

Muffled noises outside the door drew me away from quilting one Saturday. Loud thuds and soft curses led me to cautiously open the door. The sight of two men in blue pulling and tugging on a beautiful pine armoire was curious in itself but when they set it down at the door opposite mine I watched the dark-haired one slap his pockets before emitting a groan.

"How could you leave the key, Mac?" The stockier man slumped against the door.

"I'd just picked it up from the Realtor when we got that robbery call. I must have left it on the desk."

"Okay, okay, so what do we do now?"

Well, after all, they were cops. So I just spoke right up. "Do you need a phone?"

Two heads turned my way. The taller man fixed his dark gaze on me. At first, I thought he wasn't going to answer. Then in a quiet, almost cold voice he asked, "Do you always invite strange men into your home?"

"You are policemen, aren't you?" *What's with this guy?*

"What if we're impostors?" The other man attempted to follow his partner with a stern look.

"Impossible." I laughed. "No fake cops would lug a hundred pound plus piece of furniture upstairs."

We all laughed then. Mac . . . Sgt. Theodore MacDonald . . . left his partner in the hall as I pointed to the phone on the kitchen wall. It sounded like someone at the station house promised to bring the key to the loft across the hall which Mac had closed escrow on. From my place at the front door, I watched him on the phone. Square jaw, thick wavy hair, naturally tanned from the outdoors. . .whew, neighbors like him were dangerous to the mental state of a woman who had so recently been tossed aside.

"This is beautiful." He stopped beside the quilt frame after turning from the phone. "Is this your work?"

"A labor of love."

"It's art." He looked around the room at all of the quilts and pieces hung on the wall. When he walked over to the one laid across the back of the sofa, he ran a large hand across it ever so gently. "Do you sell?"

"No." I'd never even given a thought to parting with my pretties.

For a moment I thought he would ask for a reason. But when I met his eyes I found acceptance there and something else, respect maybe. "I'm interested, if you ever change your mind. You know where to find me."

Over the next weeks I saw Mac several times coming or going, both of us in a hurry for one destination or the other. His shifts seemed to change often; his days off must have been on days I was away. One Sunday I did see him in the park jogging. In spite of the fact that I was sick and tired of jogging on a treadmill, I might have joined him if I had been asked. And if I had encouraged him to stop he might have invited me. I didn't and he didn't.

I invited Sandy over for a light lunch on the weekend after I weighed in twenty pounds lighter than my old self. At the door, her mouth literally hung open.

Then she squealed, "I hardly recognize you!"

I felt real sorry for Sandy, even though I don't think that I would ever say that to her. She's one of those women we all know, the one who has been told all her life that she has a pretty face. She knows, I'm sure she really knows, what they mean – she does have a lovely face but she would be a real beauty if she'd lose some weight. I, her friend since before high school, couldn't tell her that she should join me at the Diet Bar.

"Thanks, Sandy. That makes me feel real good. I still have a few more pounds to meet my goal. Then I'll buy some new clothes. These nipped-in, tucked-up clothes are not exactly a fashion statement." That drew a laugh from Sandy as she eyed the baggy pants I wore. "I haven't been avoiding you, but have been spending most of my time at the Diet Bar or library."

"I've been busy, too. Charley had business trips to Chicago and Dallas, both of which I could take with him."

We caught up on the local gossip, what was happening with her family and had almost finished the Caesar salad with Cajun grilled chicken strips when she dropped the hot potato in my lap.

"Uh, Kelly, I don't know how to tell you this . . ." She seemed really stressed over whatever she wanted to say.

"Spit it out, honey."

"Jerry called me last week. He's. . .well, it seems he's . . . I think Trish has dumped him."

"Really!" I let a big grin take over my whole face. "Isn't that just too bad?" I could afford a little sarcasm here.

"He wanted to know where you lived now. I couldn't tell him because, until you called with your lunch invitation, I didn't actually have an address. Not that I couldn't have found out the exact apartment number." She grinned. "And your phone number is unlisted. I didn't tell him that I talk to you often but I could honestly say that I hadn't seen you."

"How sad." I laughed.

"He was pretty persistent."

"If I see him, I'll just tell him to get lost. Why would he want to hear that?"

"I hope you mean that." Sandy studied me closely.

"What are you trying to say, Sandy?"

"I just worry maybe you've pushed yourself at such a fast pace – you know, trying to forget Jerry, losing all that weight, making so many other changes in your life – that maybe you're just fooling yourself into believing you're really over him, happy and all that."

"Honey, listen to me closely." I placed my hand over hers. "I am happy. I'm settled in nicely here. I love my new life, this place I've nested in, even my job at the library. I have no intentions of ever going back to the old life – especially not to Jerry."

"He's very determined."

"Stop worrying, Sandy. When I do see him, I'll take care of it."

I didn't have to wait too long. Rounding the end of the aisle in Jax Market, I literally ran into Jerry.

For a moment he just stood there. I could tell by the look on his face that it was quite a shock to see me, pounds lighter, decked out in a short red knit dress, my hair streaked with blonde

 highlights. I felt something I could easily recognize as a gloat begins to bubble up. After all, the sweetest revenge is getting skinny.

"My, my, look at you." He finally said, staring at me with that look he used to get before he was going to say something I was supposed to really appreciate hearing. "I'm not with Trish anymore." Man, that was getting right to the point.

"I heard." I turned away from him, picking out ripe peaches, placing them in a bag.

"Yeah, uh, I'm really sorry for any embarrassment I caused you. It was crazy of me to let you go."

"Let me go?" Was he just waiting to see me lose my cool here? "You walked out on me for another woman. It was degrading and, yes, humiliating, to finally understand that you were more interested in skinny flesh than heavy caring."

"Ah, Kelly, it was just a mid-life thing."

"Oh, yeah?" I curled my lips around the words. "Tough! I've gone beyond playing those little games."

"I want to come back." Had I never noticed how Jerry whined when things weren't going his way?

"Don't you get it?" I began to move away from him, pushing the cart toward the checkout stand. "Our divorce will be final in a matter of days. And that's what it will be, Jerry. Final. Finis. Quits. We'll both be able to go on with our lives."

"Ah, honey, you can't just throw away all we had."

"You did that months ago, didn't you?" When I tried to move into the line, Jerry stepped in front of the cart. I ground my teeth together. "Get out of my way. Leave me alone. No calls, no knocks on the door, no visits to my job, nothing."

"I won't allow this." This tactic I had heard before, too.

"I mean what I say, Jerry. If you ever come near me again, I'll call a cop." An image of Mac floated through my mind as I spoke the words. "I just happen to know a good one."

Jerry was no where in sight when I came out of the store to place the bags of groceries in the trunk of my old Blue Honda. I drove home, grinning like an idiot, humming along with "Yesterday" by the Beatles, playing softly on the "oldies" station. As I pulled into my assigned parking space in the underground garage I noticed Mac's Bronco was in its place. In my mind I began to run through the completed quilt patterns – Wild Goose Chase, Texas Star, maybe even the one I had just completed, Flower Garden.

I think it's okay now to talk about selling a quilt.

~

SUNBONNET SUE

"You're never going to see another sunrise! You've screwed with me for the last time! I've tried to keep you from messing up. But you just keep right on doing everything wrong! I've had it with you! Stupid bitch! I'm going to kill you!"

She knew what was coming. It wouldn't be a fist or cigarette burns or an arm twisted. Tonight Brad had gone over the edge. She could see it in his bloodshot eyes. He meant to kill her. Grace meant to live. Too many times she hadn't sought help, hadn't pressed charges against him for his cruelty. In the past he'd cried, said he was sorry, made worthless promises. This time she wasn't going to stand still. This time she would protect herself.

Brad lunged for her. At the same moment Gracie lifted her hand to ward off the blow, she pulled the gun from the drawer. The sound of the one shot would echo in her head forever. A little after 3 a.m. the police found her huddled on a neighbor's porch wearing only a long T-shirt. She was bleeding, bruises were coloring on her arms, neck, legs. One eye was swollen shut.

Grace was arrested.

* * *

I'm going to die here. How many doors do you pass through before you arrive at death row?

Oiled doors on automatic tracks glide smoothly open.

Then Grace hears the clatter of the bolt interlocking with the bar, reverberating in the silence of the walk. Each clank of a lock behind her as she moves down the corridor, stepping through each access, is a little part of the overall death.

"There's still the governor, honey. Don't give up hope." The words were from Aggie. They had become friends, if a person sentenced to die dared call anyone friend, while working in the library together. There weren't many places where Grace was allowed to go but what danger could she be to books, right? A slight smile touching her mouth was the only answer to Aggie's encouragement Grace could allow herself.

Sam's with her. He's her favorite of the many guards here. He requested to sit on this watch. Grace thought he was probably someone's grandfather. Not hers for sure. All she remembered about her grandfather was the belt he used when one of his children or grandchildren misstepped. Sam was too kind for most of the tough-skinned, rough-talking women he came into contact with here but, in spite of her sentence, seemed to act as a confident when she needed one. He had promised long ago to answer her questions, especially the ones she never wanted to ask before. Sam could tell her how to die.

Grace had been given her choice for the method the State would use . . . sit on the electric chair jokingly called "Hot Mama" or lethal injection . . . a needle filled with poison silently killing her. Aggie told her the story of the last woman executed.

"Old Joely Adkins was tied down to 'Hot Mama' last year. She kicked and screamed and cussed all the way down that hallway. Always said she wasn't goin' to hell quietly. Well, the executioner pulled that switch and Joely just sat there. She refused to die."

"Electricity failed?" Grace asked despite her efforts to appear uninterested.

"Who knows? Anyway, they pulled the switch again. Smoke rose from the top of her shaved head to the bottom of her shackled feet." Aggie grinned as Grace squirmed, now noticeably uncomfortable with the story. "They left her sitting there strapped in while electricians worked on the problem."

"Shit!"

"I guess the reporters outside got word of the goin'-ons in here and broadcast it on the TV news. Someone high up gets calls that might upset his next election so he leans on the warden. Some people were cryin' out that she should be allowed to live."

"But she wasn't."

"They sent her back to the holding cell until a hearing could be staged. The courts set her back down twenty-four hours later and killed her all over again."

Grace chose the needle.

Attorneys had worked miracles these past fourteen years, keeping her from entering the green room several times. They had been so sure the courts would allow another trial on the grounds of evidence withheld. Many states were now allowing proof of spousal abuse to be used as reason for murdering the offender. But this state stood firm. "No O.J. cases in our state. There'll be no talk of that Menendez abuse-excuse in our courts."

At the end of the walk Grace stepped into a small cell. Placing her bedding and brown-paper sack down, without hesitation she quickly made her bed, tucking the corners in tight as she had learned early in her incarceration. From the sack she pulled out a framed picture and a toothbrush placing each on the rim of the stainless-steel sink hanging on the wall. The last thing she pulled out was a quilted coverlet appliquéd with bonneted figures.

"Have you finished it yet?" Sam stood in the open cell door.

"Just a few more stitches." Grace managed a wistful smile. "I hope Susan likes it."

"Sure she will, Miss Grace. That child loves having you for a stepmother. She will . . . she'll never forget you."

"I don't know that I want her to remember me, Sam. What kind of role model can I be?" Her green eyes usually so filled with hope were now sad.

"She understands why you're here and loves you in spite, or maybe because of the reason." Sam reminded her. "You're loved, Miss Grace. Deep down you know that. Making this quilt for her is a token of love. Families don't forget."

"Ah, I do know that." Grace grimaced. "Brad's father has never forgotten that I killed his son. He is longing for justice."

Sam pulled his chair to the door. "What caused all this, Miss Grace?" He flung out a hand to encompass the cell, the prison, the sentence. He watched the slender form tense. "I've only heard the official version."

After some hesitation, Grace collected herself enough to answer. "One of those old stories you've heard before, Sam. I married Brad after a whirlwind courtship. He was Mr. Charming, swept me right off my feet. The honeymoon was over the first time I questioned his authority, as he called it."

"He was abusive?"

"Continuously. Verbally – I couldn't do anything right. Couldn't cook or clean or dress or speak the way Brad thought proper. Then he began to slap me. The first time he struck me I was dumfounded. I just couldn't believe that was happening to me. Of course, he made sure that I thought it was my fault."

"What changed your mind?"

"Brad broke my nose and cracked some ribs. He wouldn't take me to the hospital. Told me I shouldn't have provoked him with my stupidity. So I drove myself. The doctors patched me up and suggested, rather strongly if I remember right, that I get out. On my way home I found myself stopping at St. Michael's."

"They say prayer soothes all pain."

"I hadn't asked God for anything in a long time but I prayed for hours. I figured I had God's answer when I arrived home. Brad picked up right where he had left off. I thought God had forsaken me just as I had ignored Him for all those years."

Sam sat quietly, his eyes puddling with tears, until Grace began speaking again.

"He roughed me up again and something snapped. I was in pain from those previous injuries. I don't remember getting the gun from it's hiding place, but the shot startled me. I panicked and took off."

"That's why the police weren't called right away?"

"I ran . . . I don't know how many blocks. Then I went back." Grace shuddered. "I couldn't touch him. But I knew he was dead. I went to the neighbor's and asked them to dial 911. Then I waited for the police to come get me."

"And then the trial where they found you guilty?"

"It was all cut and dried as far as the prosecutor was concerned. Without allowing pictures of my injuries, the report from the hospital, listening to witnesses to Brad hitting me . . . well, you can see where a jury would see me as a woman who set out to kill her husband. I don't know what the motive was supposed to be but prosecutors don't have to prove motive, do they?"

Grace slipped the needle in and out of the comforter, following the outline of the little girl in bonnet with small neat stitches. Sam moved his chair back to the desk, leaving her with her work, her thoughts, her guilt.

She gently touched the frame holding the dear smiling faces of a good man and his beautiful child. She couldn't see the lovely twelve-year old again. It would break hearts, especially hers. Doug, the forgiving, loving man who had come into her life because he wanted to write a book about a woman on death row, had insisted on meeting her when she showed reluctance. Grace had managed to stay strong through the last few days . . . until Doug came for his last visit. She had broken down completely and they had spent that precious time wiping away each other's tears, saying their good-byes over and over again. *I mustn't think about that anymore. I have work to finish.*

Sam came to her at nine. Grace knew from the grim look that the last appeal to the governor had failed. "Time to go, huh, Sam?"

She shared her last meal with him. Pepperoni pizza, Caesar salad, Dr. Pepper. She wondered what those reporters outside would make of that. Then Sam left her alone with her minister for an hour of prayer. Will the outside world find something sinister about that?

It was time. Too soon.

Grace folded the comforter and placed in the large bag. On top of her belongings she laid the photograph of Doug and Susan, then handed it all to Sam.

"Please see that Doug receives this, will you, Sam?"

"I sure will." Sam's eyes reflected the sorrow he felt.

It was a short walk to the green room. The ugly "Hot Mama" stood in the same room with a gurney nearby. The curtains were drawn over the viewing windows as Grace entered the room. She was quickly strapped down, a doctor slipped the needle into the proper vein with an attached tube running down and out of sight, waiting for the shut-off valve to be flipped, allowing the lethal cocktail to slowly end her life. It was only after she was in place that the curtains were opened.

Grace wouldn't turn her head to see Brad's father who she knew was there to make sure she died. She didn't want the past to be the last thing she saw. She immediately caught Doug's eye. Even with tears on his cheeks he managed a smile as he blew her a kiss, lifting the quilted comforter up for her to see. She met his look with a weak smile of her own, then mouthed "I love you," before closing her eyes.

Jesus, I prayed you would never forget me and, in my final hours, You have shown Your love for Your sinful child. Thank you for blessing me with Doug and Susan. But was it a sin to love them so? Forgive me for the years that I closed myself off from you. Was that an unforgivable sin?

Please, God, forgive me for the breaking of Your commandment – Thou Shalt Not Kill. Will that keep me from Your heavenly kingdom?

Oh, Lord, please tell me – which one of my sins am I being executed for?

~

TRIP AROUND THE WORLD

"But his parents are dead. How can a government deny an orphaned child the chance for a home?" In frustration, Andrew combed fingers through his close-cropped hair.

"You cannot take him with you, Mrs. Bruce," the agent for America's Hands to Vietnam reminded Carol, ignoring Andrew's comment. "All of the papers have been filed but the officials here often take a year to sign them."

"So what you're telling me is that in the meantime, the boy lives here in an institution where he doesn't get enough to eat, receives next to no medical care . . . and may not even be alive when we return." Andrew, who hadn't been too keen on this process at the outset, had fallen in love with three-year old Tuyen almost from their first meeting. He often grumbled that Adults fight war but it is the children who are hurt the most. Andrew wanted to take his son home now.

The agent once again ignored him. "We have arranged for you to spend the afternoon with the boy. Today you take him to the park across the street. He will be agreeable I am sure. He knows a few words of English, but I have never heard him speak . . . in any language."

The Bruces' had planned and waited for ten years to have a child of their own. It hadn't happened. Needles, medication, nor tests had produced results Carol or Andrew was willing to accept. When the couple finally understood there would be no babies, they sought help from local adoption agencies. . . who told them that people in their forties were "Not acceptable." No matter that their financial abilities offered the best any child could hope for, nor that they were willing to accept any child - they were too old.

Of course, that answer wasn't going to stop determined parents-to-be. Carol and Andrew searched the Internet and researched adoption agencies outside the U.S., starting with the nearest, Mexico. There they found tremendous resistance to allowing their abandoned children to be adopted by people from other countries. "Maybe if you were of Latin ancestry," the spokesperson had offered, in all probability simply wanting to soften the blow.

Romania had hundreds of children to offer. But....

"Remember that piece on 48 Hours or 60 Minutes or whatever the show about the couple who adopted the Romanian child? She seemed so beautiful, all smiles and eagerness. But as she grew older, she became a menace to the entire family. They took her back to her country and left her." Carol shuddered at the thought of abandoning a child, not only once, but also in this case, twice.

"Yes, but the adoptive parents found out later that they had been deceived . . . the child's mother was in a mental institution."

"And her father had died an alcoholic."

There were limits to what even desperate people could accept. A missionary sponsored by their church led them to the agency in Vietnam and the three-year old that would finally make them a family.

Tuyen was dressed in faded blue pants and a worn shirt, in an outfit much too light weight for this time of year even in Saigon. And much too large for his thin frame. Carol was sure the watery gruel fed the children each day did nothing more than keep them alive. When she took the boy out of the attendant's arms he didn't pull away, but he didn't smile or laugh either. In fact, there seemed to be no emotion at all stirring within the tiny figure, nor in the vacant eyes staring up at her....

"Hey, little guy, let's go try out the swings, okay?" Andrew touched the frail shoulder. Tuyen turned his head toward the voice then buried his face in Carol's neck.

The park was filled with leafy trees offering lots of shade. The lush green grass was soft beneath their feet and, unlike such areas back home, this one was filled with vendors - - balloons for sale, kites reaching up to the sky just waiting to tangle in the trees. Greasy food smells wafted on the air. Old men sat waiting to write a letter for those who could not do so themselves. As they walked amidst this,

Carol and Andrew noted the curious looks Tuyen gave the trees and the local people strolling around. It became apparent that the child had never been to the park. His eyes darted everywhere, following the movements, seeking out the colors. The red plastic playground equipment where other children shouted, shoved, and took their turn sliding and climbing and swinging intrigued him. And when Carol sat down in the swing and Andrew began slowly pushing them, Tuyen didn't cry out but the big round, dark eyes widened and silent tears dripped down his face.

"Stop, Andrew, he's frightened." Carol pulled the stiff child closer, patted him on the back, softly cooed to him until she felt the body relax. "Let me sit here and just hold him."

The clamor of happy voices swirled around them. Tuyen lifted his head to watch one group, then another. Ever so slowly, Carol moved again, her arms cuddling Tuyen, then gradually increased the range of motion. This time he moved his head to look up at her, no longer afraid but not showing eagerness either.

Later, as the couple attempted to play games and to entertain Tuyen, they were at a loss as to what they could do to encourage the child to display pleasure, even warmth. But he didn't cry again. And he devoured the meal of fish, vegetables and noodles they purchased from a vendor at the edge of the park.

When they took him back to the orphanage, Carol gently lifted him into the crib where, despite his age, he spent most of his time. "Hug? Can you give me a hug?" She placed his thin arms around her neck for a moment, then gave him a tight squeeze as she stroked the wispy black hair. She kissed the soft cheek. Again, she felt the tiny body stiffen, withdraw from her touch. Was he afraid of her? Or had someone abused Tuyen? The thought made her sick.

With trembling hands, Carol pulled a small folded quilt from the canvas bag she carried with her. "I've brought you something," she said. The bright yellows and reds of the quarter-rounds and center circle that created the blocks making up the Around the World" pattern was even more brilliant against the dingy sheets. "See? Here. I've embroidered your name on this block . . . T-U-Y-E-N. Let Mommy tuck you in."

Tuyen couldn't take his eyes off the quilt. His hands clutched the edge, pulling it up to his chin. He gave Carol's face a hasty glance, then moved his eyes back to the bright colors just as quickly. Tiny fingers of one hand reached down to stroke the fabric, then moved upward again to hold fast to the quilt. Long lashes swept his cheek before he looked up to hold her gaze. It was then that Tuyen offered Carol his own parting gift. He smiled.

They were at the orphanage early the next morning. Again dressed in light clothing, Carol wrapped Tuyen in the quilt before they left the building.

"Let's take him around the city," Andrew suggested. "I doubt that he's ever been out much. He'll probably be fascinated."

With a map obtained from the Embassy, a phrase book, Andrew flagged down a cyclo, the bicycle/buggy for two, and they were off. Once in the center of the old city, the couple joined the throngs of people busily going about their daily lives, the unfamiliar tones of the Vietnamese language crashing together in a raucous symphony around them.

Roaming the streets, seeing the sights and shopping for souvenirs, they pointed to the map when seeking a special spot and managed, with a few words from the phrase book, to find their way around the city and communicate with shopkeepers.

Strangers looked at them curiously, two Americans lovingly carrying this small one from their country. And no one can ignore a small child. Once when Andrew was holding Tuyen, an elderly woman stopped him with a hand on his sleeve. She shook her head, then pantomimed how he should be holding the child - in front of him, so that he could see the world from a forward position. Carol and Andrew laughed, demonstrating that they were new at this and, much to their delight, Tuyen laughed with them. And later, when a young man stopped them, offering a piece of sugary confection, the boy spoke to him, soft, mellow Vietnamese words, short and to the point if the man's smile was any indication.

"What did he say?" Carol blurted out in English, forgetting the phrase book.

With a smile, he answered, "He says that you belong to him."

"Family. He means we're his family." Carol blinked back hot tears that threatened to fall. "Will you tell him that we love him? That we will take him home with us as soon as we can."

The words must have been perfect. Tuyen grinned, kicked his feet out in front of him, and bounced up and down in Andrew's arms.

As could be expected the day filled with exploration of the new and unusual sights and sounds rushed by. Heaviness began to weigh on Carol and Andrew as they waited for a cyclo to take them and their precious cargo back to the orphanage. They both kept looking at this child who would one day be a part of their family but knowing that soon they must leave him and return home to wait for the final round of papers to be signed. It was hard to face taking him back and then having to turn away.

Carol spied the booth first. "Andrew, let's have a couple of photo's made."

The photos were the usual black and white, the poses showed goofiness the booth seemed to always bring out in people. When the three pictures on a strip popped out of the machine, Carol felt Andrew's hand on her shoulder tightens as they looked at the images. He and Carol were grinning at the camera, one head on each side of Tuyen's. But it was the child's pose that created the heart of the picture. Tuyen was giggling, his wide eyes sparkling with laughter.

Before they left that night Carol pinned one of the tiny photos to the quilt.

* * *

It was eight months before Carol and Andrew landed in Saigon again. During the cab ride to their hotel in the center of the city, they could hardly control their eagerness -- or anxieties.

"What if he's forgotten us, Andrew?" Carol had spent many sleepless nights over the months worrying that such a young child might have difficulty remembering round-eyed strangers who appeared for a few days and then simply disappeared.

"We did all we could, honey . . . you wrote every week, we sent photographs, we mailed packages once a month." He hugged her close. "We'll have the answer tomorrow."

"How can I wait until tomorrow? Can't we go by the orphanage now? Just take a look at him?"

"These people are real sticklers for rules, Carol. I don't think they would look too kindly on us just popping in. We can't let anything go wrong at the last minute. Dan Jackson from the Embassy said he'd meet us with the passport at the orphanage in the morning. We'd better let him do his job."

Carol sighed. "I know you're right, but it certainly is going to be a long night."

Dan Jackson was younger than they expected but nevertheless managed to appear fully in charge of the situation. He handed a sheath of official-looking documents to the agent, who barely glanced at them, but took a great deal of time looking at the passport issued in the name of Tuyen Andrew Bruce. Seeming satisfied at last, she signed one copy of the bundle, shoved it across the desk to Dan, and, standing with hands folded in front of her, waited.

The American official turned to Carol and Andrew with a smile, offering his hand, "Congratulations. You're the proud parents of a lively *American* son."

At that moment a door at the far end of the room opened. An attendant, dressed in white, entered with a tiny figure holding her hand. The boy was dressed in blue jeans, a light blue sweatshirt, and on his dark head perched a San Diego Padres baseball cap, all gifts sent from America, a place he'd soon learn to call his own. And in his arms he clutched the bright yellow and red quilt. His eyes widened as they found Carol and Andrew, then the boy allowed the quilt to slip from his arms. He raced across the cold stone floor before flying into their outstretched arms, shouting. . . "Mommy! Daddy! Home!"

~

BLOCKS & STARS

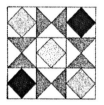

"You must be reasonable, Liz. It's one thing to volunteer for the literacy program at the Facility, but how do you think you'll get those troubled kids to pick up quilting . . . even if you can get permission to teach such a class?"

"They're bored, Jim. You know what that leads to. Restlessness. More trouble."

Liz had prayed about this long and hard. She knew somehow, some way she was going to do this. God hadn't sent her a sign that she shouldn't. But then she'd had no sign He was telling her to plow ahead either.

"What do you expect, honey?" Jim was trying to reason with his wife of thirty years. He hated to see her disappointed, but he knew this latest scheme of hers was doomed to fail. "Honey, so many of those girls are involved with gangs, rival gangs. Can you picture them? Sitting, quietly sewing, in the same room together?"

"I've managed to get them through two hours of reading without a serious rumble."

"Quilting includes scissors and needles. Someone, including you, could get seriously hurt, Liz." The concern showed on Jim's weathered face.

"That could happen, yes, but they need something else to do, Jim. A project where they can learn a craft, and so something for others, too, is a worthy goal."

Liz carried a newspaper clipping and a block of fabric done in the Log Cabin pattern with her for her appointment with Director Marshall. She offered what she knew about "Small Things", a nonprofit organization where volunteers created quilted lap robes for the elderly confined to nursing homes. Liz requested permission to teach the girls, during their free time and on a voluntary basis, of course, the craft of quilting.

"This is a sample pattern." She gave him the block. "It takes about twenty of these to make each lap robe."

"I agree they need some new interests, Mrs. Brock. I'll allow you to do this on a test basis. But if we have any dangerous incidents, I'll be forced to shut you down. And I don't have any funding for it."

In two weeks, Liz was ready to set up the classroom at one end of the cafeteria. With three sewing machines donated from church members, thread, needles, scissors provided by outlet store, and bolts and bags of fabric supplied by friends, she was ready to ask for volunteers. Making the announcement at the end of the reading session, she listened to the catcalls, chiding, hooting.

"Sewing? Hey, woman, I learned how to survive on the streets, not at home."

"None of that domestic stuff for me."

"Why should we help some old people we don't know?"

Then a voice from the back of the room silenced everyone. "I'd like to try, Mz Brock."

LaToya Williams, sentenced to the Highfield Youth Correctional Facility at age fifteen for murdering her stepfather, was notorious for the hostile attitude she continued to display three years later. She seemed to keep to herself and, because of her crime, and her large size, was left alone.

No hassling by gang members, no threats or insults by the older girls looking for a playmate to intimidate; even the officers seldom attempted to make LaToya do anything she didn't want to do. No one, least of all Liz, expected this girl to participate.

At first, only a few girls showed up. When they did, it wasn't easy to get them to settle down long enough to learn the basic principles of quilting. Several came strictly for the company of others, one definitely came to stir up trouble, but LaToya, it seemed, had come to sew.

As could be expected, trouble did erupt.

The troublemaker, LuAnne, picked up a pair of scissors in anger, LaToya jumped up and snatched them away almost immediately, and the two stood there glaring at each other. *Oh, Lord,* Liz prayed, *don't let this escalate into violence. Don't take away this program. Somehow You must work through me to reach these girls.*

"LuAnn, you don't have to be here," LaToya spit out the words, towering over one of the toughest girls in the Facility. "If you don't want to help someone outside, then stay out of here."

Silently, Liz applauded her, waiting for LuAnn's response. The girl looked at the few faces around the table, waiting, maybe hoping she'd leave the Project. Liz could almost see the anger escape; then the girl slowly turned toward her.

"Mz Brock, I - I wasn't payin' attention at first." A question was in her eyes before she spoke. "Do you think you might show me how to begin?"

"I think we could all use a refresher course, couldn't we, girls?" Liz placed an arm around the thin girl's shoulders. "There's handout sheets over there. Take one and read over it before our next meeting. That will explain a lot of what we're trying to do. Then I, or one of the others, can show you how to select your material and cut it out for the first step."

It should have been no surprise to Liz that the attendance doubled almost overnight. LuAnn, a strong leader, had dictated that this new class would be a failure. At her signal, girls filled the room at each session.

The lap robes were not perfect. Some had crooked blocks, many had irregular seamed bindings. The stitches were often too long or too short, or every size in between. But they were colorful, and warm, and created by girls once only intent on hating each other, who had come together to make something special for people who could no longer do even simple tasks for themselves.

Letters started coming in from the directors of nursing homes. Thank you's were tacked on the wall. Then pictures arrived showing frail people with wonderful smiles on their faces, each holding a precious gift.

Liz arrived at the class one day with stacks of books in her arms. "Girls, I've been thinking that this Log Cabin pattern can get pretty boring after you have made so many of them. What about a new pattern, something more challenging? I brought these books for you to look through and choose from."

Later, she sat at her table watching the girls, braids, corn rows, Afro's, ponytails, all huddled closely together over each book. There was giggling and some shoving, and then there were whispers. LaToya raised her hand.

"Mz Brock, you know, every organization has a name. Can't we have one?"

"That's an excellent idea, LaToya. Do you girls have something in mind?"

They all nodded, but it was once again LaToya who spoke for the group. "We like making these quilts for old folks, but . . . well, we'd like to make some gifts for our families, too."

"And maybe we could keep some blocks for a wall hanging in our cell," another girl offered.

"It would mean we'd have to have more time, another session during the week. Do you think you could do that, Mz Brock?"

Thank you, Lord, Liz silently whispered before she answered. "I'm sure I can find time, girls, but it has to be okayed by Director Marshall."

Hoorays rent the air. When they finally settled down, Liz had a question of her own. "And have you chosen a name? A new pattern?"

There were laughs and grins and nudges as they nodded. LaToya held up a picture of a pattern. The center of the pattern was a star with small diamonds, and more small blocks on their sides at each corner.

"It's called 'Blocks and Stars'. We want that to be our new pattern, and our name. We think it'd be a good symbol of who we are - and what we do - and what we can be someday."

"You think there's a certain symbolism in this pattern for you?"

"Yes, ma'am." A chorus of voices answered.

Spokesperson LaToya went on. "The blocks are a sign - symbol, as you called it - of our cell blocks, places we all plan not to see again once we leave here."

"Good depiction." Liz smiled at the faces surrounding her, joy rising up to fill her. *Your lessons learned, Lord.* "And the stars?"

One said, "We're reaching for the stars."

"The stars are high, bright, free," another shouted.

"With these quilts, that's what we've become to some old folks . . . stars." This from the girl who once asked why any one of them would want to do anything for some old people they didn't even know.

There were cheers when Liz agreed with them that "Blocks and Stars" was an excellent choice for their group name, and for a new pattern. And she knew that each of them, in a certain special way, had become a star.

The quilts, and God's healing, had been the thread that created a common bond between the least of the world's children.

~

JOSEPH'S COAT

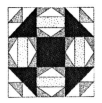

Josefina knelt in her pew while the voices of the small choir singing the *Gloria* flowed around her. She looked forward to her time in church, especially Sunday Mass. The Padre looked so regal with the broad gold vestment around his neck gleaming against the pristine while of his robe. Later, when the voices of the congregation were raised to recite the novena, Josefina would sense even more the reverence of the day and place.

There had been no church in her tiny village in Chiapas. The Federales, in their quest to control the Indians who protested starvation, lack of a voice in their government and ill treatment in general, had burned the church to the ground. The Padre had escaped into the jungle but each Sunday he held services somewhere; in a cave in the mountains, down by the river or under shade trees in the valley. Of course it wasn't the same without the statues of Jesus and the Virgin Mary around her and when word came that her husband and eldest son had been "eliminated" by the soldiers, her remaining son, Oscar, had suggested they go to the States.

Josefina had gasped. "Estados Unidos! So far away? Oh, no, mi hijo."

"Mamacita, what do you have here?" Oscar had thrown out his hand to indicate the poor hovel they called home, the garden she must now work alone in order for them to eat, the village almost emptied of all her friends and family. "Wouldn't you like to have a real church again?"

That promise sent her on the dangerous trek across the Yucatan to find a coyote that would take all the money they possessed and deposit them in a fast-paced alien city north of the Rio Grande. Sanctuary had been found in this hundred-year old, high-ceilinged adobe church in a Mexican colonia. Here they were provided with a bed on the floor of the recreation room with others like them, and food for both her spirit and her belly. When Oscar found permanent work they could move on and make room for the next unfortunates.

And for several months Oscar had been able to find work, though he didn't make enough money for them to move on. It allowed them to give a little to this church for their shelter and some to the Ladies Altar Society for the food provided. Then one night Oscar brought her news that set her heart to pounding.

"The I.N.S. made a sweep through the shop today, Mamacita. Manuel and I barely escaped by squeezing through the bathroom window. It is not safe to work in a border city."

"What will we do? We have no money to go back."

"Back?" Oscar spit out the word, dark eyes flashing at her. "I will never go back. Manuel says we can find work with the crops in what they call "The Valley." We leave tomorrow."

Though it hurt to think of leaving, she accepted the reasoning behind Oscar's decision. "I will gather our things. I must speak to the Padre, thank him for his kindness." Josefina reached for the shopping bags that would hold their meager possessions. Oscar reached out to still her hands.

"I must go alone, Mamacita."

"Alone?" Josefina looked at him in confusion, fear inside growing. "But you said we must always. . .how do they say it here? Stick together?"

"These farms only take men, Mamacita." His eyes were now filled with sadness. "Manuel says the men follow the crops. We may go as far away as California."

"California? No, mi hijo, that is too far. And it is said the Migra look always for you there." Her eyes filled with tears for she knew that he would go. "But what will I do?"

"As soon as I can I will send money. Wait a few days, then go to the Padre and explain. He will understand."

Josefina had not gone to the Padre right away. After service today, she must find the courage to approach him. Each day she had come here among the old ladies who said the rosary out loud, to pray for Manuel, her village, herself. She knelt before Jesus, the Madre, then her special saint, The

Lady of Guadalupe, asking each for a sign that it was the right time to talk to the Padre. And she asked to hear soon from Oscar. After lunch she sought out the Padre in his tiny office in the rectory. "Padre, I must ask for your forgiveness."

The Padre frowned at her from behind the large desk. "But I heard your confession, Josefina. What more could you have to say?"

"Mi hijo, Oscar, has gone away for work." She paused, then taking a deep breath went on, "I have no money to pay for my bed or food, Padre."

The Padre had seen so many of these young men go off to work in the hot sun for low pay, not earning enough to make a proper life for themselves much less anyone else. It saddened him to hear that another son had been forced to seek that path.

"That has never been a problem here, Josefina." The Padre's flushed Irish face was creased in a smile. "You only paid when you could. That money allows us to help someone else but the lack of it does not mean that you cannot stay."

"Gracias, Padre, but . . ." Josefina was becoming agitated. "That is not my way. I must do something."

"Ah, yes, I see." He studied the Indian woman before him, black hair braided in one large plait hanging down her back, colorful clothing of her region patched but always clean, worn hands he had often seen clasped in prayer. She had lost everything that mattered. The least he could do was guarantee that at least her pride be left intact. "Let me speak to the Ladies Altar Society. Surely there is work for you there. I can't promise you any money, Josefina, but we will find something for you to do that will pay for your place here."

She had been given the job of keeping the altar clean and set up for services. She had found great pleasure in removing years of grim from the statues, in seeing the soft beauty of features and garments returned. And so it was that Josefina found herself in Sunday Mass at the beginning of the holiday season acknowledging that the special arrangement of poinsettias around the shining statues was due to her efforts. The Mexican Christmas flowers were provided by the more prosperous members of the Parish. but Josefina's eye for beauty had artistically placed them around the front of the church.

Janitors brought the life-size Nativity pieces out of storage and arranged them on one side of the altar. Josefina found herself among the worshipers at the end of the service going forward to kneel before the Christ Child. She sees that other people are leaving tokens of their love. . . a sprig of flowers, a lighted scented candle but mostly money.

Josefina's thoughts were on that blessed birth, how much hope it had brought to the whole world, even the poor people like herself who had escaped evil men in power. She wanted to make a contribution to this Holy Family but how? She had no money, nothing. *If Oscar would write, could send a little money* . . . no, she mustn't count on that.

She studied the Nativity closely. The baby Jesus laid swaddled in his white cloth, on a rough-hewn manager filled with hay. Madre Maria kneeled beside him in her soft, saintly blue garments. Her husband, Joseph, stood looking down on his son, his clothes the non-color beige of a man of modest means. A plan began to form in Josefina's mind.

Day care for both the elderly and children was offered in the recreation hall during the day. Josefina had volunteered her time when not cleaning to assist the Ladies Altar Society women with the crafts they taught to keep both ages busy. It was in their supplies that she found the materials needed for her project.

She only worked on her gift after her other tasks were completed. At night while the others slept she used a borrowed flashlight to work an extra hour with her needle on cloth. During the day Josefina found time to fit and adjust her present. And then it was done.

Josefina knelt in her pew clutching the missal, which held a precious gift. On this day she had received a lovely Christmas card, all in flowing Spanish, from Oscar, postmarked somewhere called Cherokee, Oklahoma. He had no work for the winter but he and Manuel had saved enough to survive until the next crop was to be harvested. No money for her but Josefina praised God that Oscar was safe and that he wasn't in that California place. She had so much to be thankful for on this eve of Christ's birth.

As the crowds filled the church pews for Midnight Mass, they were greeted with the beauty of the altar, flaming candles throughout the church, the sandalwood scent of incense used now only on special Holy Days, and a most unusual sight! The Nativity scene had a most colorful addition.

Serene as always in her beauty, Mary gazed down on her son who had been sent to save the world from its wickedness. The baby, feet raised in a typical kicking position, seemed happy in his poor bed. But it was Joseph that called out for attention this night.

Draped around his shoulders was a coat of many colors, its diagonal pattern inside small blocks seeming to push out against each other. It was certainly the most beautiful quilted covering anyone, especially the papier-mâché Joseph, had ever owned.

Josefina listened to the whispers around her. Some said it was wonderful. Another said it wasn't very Holy but it sure got everyone's attention. Josefina wasn't worried about what others thought. The Padre had said it was magnificent, a robe justly earned by a father such as Joseph, one who had accepted the miracle God had bestowed on both he and Mary. And Josefina knew that this father would be remembered on every Christmas because of her gift.

Feasting her eyes on all the glory before her, Josefina's thoughts rushed forward. Maybe next year. . . What about a quilted mantilla for the Holy Madre? Or a crib quilt for the Blessed Child? As she knelt in her pew, Josefina knew she had much necessary work left to do.

~

WEATHER VANE

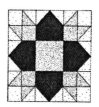

Mama found me a pair of gloves, the old parka trimmed in fur, and boots left in the mudroom. All were too large. They must have been Jake's.

"The stock needs water and some grain, Sarah. You'd better go." Mama directed me, though she glanced at the door off the kitchen where daddy lay asleep under a heavy pile of quilts. *If she's waiting for any support she was wasting her efforts.*

"I haven't ridden in years." I had never been able to string words into protests or complaints when aimed at either of my parents. Never a refusal.

"There's no one else to do it."

No way would mama ever think of leaving her warm cozy kitchen to lift a helping hand outdoors. When Lelia Cross, a teenager from a miner's shack in Dawson married Warren Tate, the eldest son of a prosperous rancher in Paradise Valley, she vowed never to chop another piece of wood, milk another cow, or dig another potato. She'd kept her word.

I didn't want to be here. I have a wonderful

apartment not far from the beach in a small Southern California town, a job I love at the newspaper and I had never planned to come back to the ranch, at least not in the dead of winter. It had taken me ten years to get up the nerve to leave. There had been such guilt; Jake dying, me being the only child left. But I'd made it through college and found my way into a life of my own. I wanted to keep it that way.

That call had frightened me. And that made me feel guilty, too. For I feared for Daddy's health, and mine. I was scared to death that I'd be caught up in my parents needs, enlarge on those old guilts that hadn't truly died, be held to the "duties" of a child.

"I'll scare the cows into a stampede dressed like this," I grumbled as I lifted the latch and pulled the back door open, catching the first blast of Wyoming winter in my face. I gulped in ice.

"Breathe through your nose or you'll freeze-burn your lungs." Mama yelled above the wind, as if she really knew what it felt like to brave the cold to do chores. I tucked my head into the fur collar and headed for the barn.

I had been warm and busy when the phone rang two days ago. I knew something had happened when I heard the voice come across the line. I was sitting at the same desk where mama had called to tell me that Jake had been killed in Da Nang. I had rushed home then, too, only to stand in shocked silence as a flag-draped bronze casket was lowered into the dark earth, taking away my only brother, my best friend, my shining dead hero.

At least this call hadn't contained the word death but it might just as well have. Daddy had suffered a heart attack and stroke leaving him paralyzed on one side and unable, or unwilling, to speak. I came home to find him ignoring us, refusing to even open his eyes when either of us spoke to him and mama walking around in a daze with glimpses of wild fear in her eyes.

California skies had been filled with bright sunshine, the sound of birds flitting around in the pepper trees, a soft ocean breeze making the wind chimes sing. Wyoming's skies were gunmetal gray, distant mountains were white, the wind was fierce and bitter, the temperature was forty below. I had to pull off the gloves to make quick work of saddling Curly, the one horse I knew wouldn't throw me. Foggy breath shrouded our heads as I slipped a small ax into the rifle scabbard. Then, with a large bag of pressed feed cakes tied behind the saddle, I mounted.

Curly seemed broader, taller, than I remembered. He snorted in the cold air and began to trot, hooves sounding loud on the frozen ground of the pasture. The horse seemed to know, even if I could only guess, where we would find the herd of cattle. At the end of a broad meadow I found them huddled beneath a stand of naked trees. Hereford steers, red coats outstanding against the pristine snow, in unison turned faces toward me. As I slid from the saddle and fumbled with the gunny sack, I could hear and feel their movement. I knew there were no bulls among them and, ordinarily, they were gentle animals. But as they drew closer and closer I could hear strange sounds, almost like moans, coming from thick slobbering lips. Steam floated from broad nostrils, uncharacteristically flared. *Was I going to be in trouble here?*

Huge shoulders and heavy heads pressed against me seeking the feed in the sacks I clutched tightly to my chest. Before I could turn to pour the cakes into the feed bin they surged forward again, pushing me off balance. I flung the sack away from my body as I fell, grazing the side of my face on the side of the trough.

Trembling, I wound my arms around myself watching the cattle push at each other now, shoving their bulk against each other, sparring over the spilled food. Before they could finish I retrieved the ax and broke up the ice in the water tube. A jagged piece of ice caught my wrist and, for a moment, I watched the blood drip down inside my glove.

I don't know which weighed heaviest on me, the clothes or the cold, but I struggled to get back up on Curly. Then, as if he knew that a warm barn awaited him, the impatient horse wheeled around, lowered his neck and, body stretched out, and galloped off toward the ranch house.

He's going to kill us both. I clutched the reins and saddle horn. Wind bit at my cheeks and nose. Ice formed as my eyes watered. If Curly slipped in the icy pasture or stepped into a gopher hole, we'd both die out here.

With relief the barn soon appeared through the gathering darkness. Curly jerked to a stop and I gratefully slipped off his back. Too weary to swing the saddle up, I dropped it on the floor of the barn, quickly rubbed the horse down and led him into his stall. I barely managed to pour feed out as exhaustion began taking it's toll on me, sending my thoughts in a tumble.

Please, God, don't let them take my freedom away.

I know mama is scared, too. She's lost without daddy; he's always been her friend, her husband, and her protector. He made her feel like a queen all the years she had been his wife. I had once been in that mining town, could see that most women born there never found their way out. She'd been what he wanted, always would be and if daddy didn't recover she was faced with making a new life for herself. Her freedom would be taken away, too.

On the back porch I found a kettle of warm water waiting beside the old tin wash pan. In the yellow light of the bare bulb, I caught a glimpse of my reflection in the cracked mirror daddy always shaved by. The scrape on the side of my face looked nasty. Beneath it was a puffy spot beginning to turn the purple of a new bruise. Gently, I washed the blood and grime off my face and arm, then turned to seek the warmth of the kitchen.

The fragrance of simmering soup and fresh-baked biscuits greeted me. Mama set at one end of the table with her small hoop on a stand holding a piece she was quilting.

"Another one for Murphy's Antiques?"

"Not this one." She turned it so that I could see dusty roses, blues and soft greens making up the assorted shapes of the Weather Vane pattern.

"It's lovely." My bones ached as I sat down near her with a bowl of soup. "You do such beautiful work, Mama."

"I thought you might need something colorful for your apartment."

I was so surprised I could only sit there motionless. "It's mine? But, Mama, I thought . . ."

"I appreciate that you came home to help out, Sarah, but you have a life back in California, people who depend on you, a job you deserve. We'll be fine. Daddy just needs a little healing." She patted my hand. "One day, when the ranch is yours, you'll have to choose where your heart truly belongs."

Tears stung my eyes. "Oh, Mama . . ."

Maybe I didn't have the right words to tell her how much my other life meant to me but somehow she understood. At that moment I did realize that for now I was where I needed to be.

"Sarah?"

We both stiffened at the sound of the scratchy voice coming from the bedroom. I shoved my empty bowl back, stiffly rose from the chair, then moved to the doorway.

Daddy was propped up against the pillows. Pale and drawn, he seemed fragile in the flannel pajamas hanging on his thin frame. He raised piercing blue eyes to meet mine. Silently we studied each other. When he managed to slowly extend his hand, I rushed forward.

That quick hug felt good. I kept his hand in mine as I sat on the side of the bed. "How are you feeling, Daddy?"

He made an attempt to speak, garbled the sounds, and then balled his free hand in a fist of frustration. He shook his head, then reached up to touch my bruises, a question in his eyes.

I made my voice sound light. "Between shoving hungry cows and Curly jolting me almost to pieces, I had quite a time trying to play cowgirl."

He smiled, then managed a few stumbling words. "Always. . .liked. . .to ride."

For a moment I didn't know whether to laugh or cry. Then, from deep within where I tucked all the good memories of this life and my family, I pulled up a shaky smile. "I guess it's no worse than riding the LA freeways."

A laugh rumbled in his chest. I marveled at the sound. Then squeezing my hand with his slight strength, he said, "Good. . .here. . .now." He tried to sound stern. "Then. . .go back. . .home."

~

3' X 6'

"Joe, it's Meg," I called out as I opened the door. "Food's here." My heart began to pound against my ribs as I listened to the silence. "Are you okay?"

"A little slow today." His voice was barely audible from where I stood.

"I'll have it ready in just a minute." I said loudly as I headed for the small apartment's kitchen.

Setting the thermal box on the dinette table, I quickly hung my purse on the back of a chair and busied myself with placement of the hot food on one of Joe's prized china plates. Adding a glass and diet drink to the tray, I hurried to the bedroom.

There had been good days when Joe met me at the door, clean-shaven, dressed immaculately in slacks and sweater, and filled with quick words tinted with his cheeky one-liners. I always delivered his evening meal last on my "Mama's Kitchen" route, so that we could sit in his sunny kitchen while he ate and I sipped a cup of raspberry tea.

This was not going to be one of those pleasant days. He looked weaker. A shadow of beard clung to the lean jaw and the usual bright spark in the brown eyes was a dull glimmer today. Flannel pajamas were unthinkable in

August, but Joe's thin frame required warmth. I could swear that his cheeks had sunken since Friday's smile had greeted me. Was it just a bad day, or something more?

"Has Karen been in?" His Hospice nurse was assigned to visit, check Joe's state of health for the day and aide in tasks that he might not be able to do for himself.

"Had a bath and my medication." He ran a shaky hand across his face. "Said she'd be back for the shave. Got beeped for some emergency."

I plumped up the pillows and raised the bed so he could eat. "Can I do anything else?"

"Talk?"

"Sure." I settled down beside the bed, watching him pick at the food on his plate.

"I talked to Mom today."

I held my breath, hope rising in me. Joe had been estranged from his parents since he became ill enough that he felt he must tell them about his disease.

"Is she coming to visit?"

I knew the answer when his eyes filled with tears. "She wants to, but . . . but Dad won't allow it."

I wanted to scream at his parents. Why couldn't they understand that Joe's lifestyle had nothing to do with his contracting AIDS, that a blood transfusion changed his life forever? How could a mother not be strong enough to ignore the dictates of a father who refused his son the love and support he needed at such a time? How could a father dismiss the fine man his son had become? Oh, God, I want to shake those people. I wanted to do something, anything, to make him feel better. I wanted to say something . . . but I could only remain silent.

Seeming to sense that I wanted to hear more, Joe said, "You know how it is with people, Meg." He sat, rigid anger tinting his cheeks. "The gays don't want me! The straight people are afraid of me! No one wants to deal with this disease. So . . . I do the best I can, alone . . . except for you." He eased himself back on the pillow, the fight gone out of him.

We had had this conversation before, and I never could add anything that would help. Now, I waited for him to continue. "You know many people think I brought this on myself by a certain kind of lifestyle. I even have to fight the insurance companies for the right to use my health care, and it took three attempts to be placed on disability even though I could no longer work." His thoughts brought out a dry chuckle. "If I was gay and had a lover, I would have someone to care for me, wouldn't I?"

Listening to Joe made me want to flatten someone with my bare fists but left me at a loss for words as usual. Just as I would have picked up the tray, Joe spoke again. "I want to thank you for this." Joe's long, bony fingers stroked the patterns of bright yellows, soft pinks, and leafy green fabrics making up the nine-patch quilt I had sewn for him.

Quilting was an obsession with me. Each of my family and friends eventually received one of my creations.

"You've already thanked me too many times, Joe. Making it for you was my pleasure."

"Would you think I was real pushy if I asked you to quilt me something else?"

"Pushy? Well, maybe . . ." I grinned down at him. "But you can always ask."

"Have you heard about the AIDS quilt?"

I could feel the chill creep through my body. "I saw a short documentary about it on TV once."

He leaned over and picked up a folder from the bedside table. "I've done some research on the Internet about this Names Project group that began the whole thing back in 1987. Did you know that there are over 41,000 individual panels now? They can't display the quilt in one place so portions are sent around the country."

"That's amazing." I glanced at the colored pictures of the pieces.

"Will you quilt me a memory panel, Meg?"

I never allowed myself to cry over Joe. At least not where he could see me. But he got to me with his request. We both knew that time was running out, had even touched on the subject now and then, but never dwelled on it. Now, with this work, Joe was bringing the future right into the here and now. It would be one of the hardest things I ever tried to do, but how could I refuse?

I shoved the tray table out of the way in order to reach down and hug the frail body, eyes spilling over with salty tears. "Oh, Joe, of course I will. It would be an honor."

He wiped his eyes on his sleeve, as if wanting to erase the emotions that seemed so close to the surface now. Then he thrust the files at me. "You'd better take all of this material and read it over for specifications . . . . Maybe it'll be too difficult."

"The hardest part will be you deciding on a pattern and fabrics." I squeezed his hand. "We can do anything you like but you have to make a sketch of what you want the panel to look like. Then we'll discuss the materials needed. And, you'll need some lessons in quilting." I left him laughing at the thought.

It took a week of visits with sketches and discussion and samples of cloth going back and forth before Joe agreed we had a design. Over the weekend I purchased all the supplies and Monday morning we began.

On good days, we worked on his dinette over a cutting board, then laying the pieces out in the design. It looked good against the blue background. When we both agreed it was a go, I showed Joe how to baste the squares, circles, triangles, and strips in place. Then we stitched the blocks together. I tacked the top piece to the layers of backing and filler, then clamped the panel into my small quilting frame placed on a stand near Joe's bed.

"Ready to quilt, Joe?" I asked as I removed the tray on my next visit.

He gave a small snort. "You know I can't quilt."

"You helped stitch those pieces down and put the blocks together. You just use smaller stitches. Here. I'll show you."

Surprisingly, Joe was quite adept at creating the tiny neat stitches necessary to quilt. I left the frame up and encouraged him to work on it when I couldn't be there. It gave him a goal each day and he enthusiastically showed me what he had accomplished when I delivered his meals. One day he told me that he had mentioned the quilt to his mother during the weekly call she managed to make when his father wasn't at home. I listened but, as before, I didn't question Joe about their conversation.

I always found him in bed now. The work he managed to do on the project was less and less until the day I arrived to find he had done nothing. He no longer had the strength to even lift the needle and, in my heart, I knew he would not be able to finish the task. But I couldn't take it away. For when I sat there and worked on the pieces, Joe's face had a special glow as he watched the colorful design become deeply etched onto his panel.

The call from the Hospice came late one evening. I broke all speed limits to reach Joe. Karen had made him as comfortable as possible. A young priest had been in earlier to offer whatever spiritual care Joe was prepared to accept. When I kissed the sunken cheek, closed eyes quickly popped open. Squeezing his hand in mine, I leaned closer so he could see me and when his eyes focused, a sweet smile caressed his face.

"I. . .I waited for you," he whispered. "Promise. . ."

"Promise what, Joe?"

"F . . finish my mem . . memory . . ." His voice faltered.

"I'll finish it, Joe." My tears dropped on his neck. "Your panel will be a part of the quilt. I promise."

A pleased look filled the hollows of his cheeks. His gaze held mine until he closed his eyes again, took a deep breath, and I felt the pressure of his fingers fade away.

The machine answered when I called his parents. The Foresters could not come to the phone . . . I left the message that their son's memorial service would be on Monday. I knew I could call back until I reached them, but I was afraid. I didn't want to hear their real words, the cold syllables of rejection.

That Monday was a celebration of life. Many of the people who came were ones Joe had met after he was diagnosed, people who had been touched by this man who forgave those who condemned him, and offered love to those who chose to be a part of a difficult time. A class of students he had once spoken to on the subject of tolerance and forgiveness arrived; clean-cut children who understood and accepted Joe for the man he was, not the disease he had. When they sang On the *Wings of a Snow White Dove* we all wept, then found ourselves smiling, clapping our hands, joining in with the words to *I'll Fly Away*.

Joe's memory quilt was finished. The week before the arrival of the Names Project group, I thought about calling Joe's mother. Then I dismissed the idea. When I had called about his death and no one from his family had attended the memorial, their statement couldn't have been any louder.

Saturday's sea fog burned off early. By the time I arrived at the park where the AIDS Memorial Quilt was being laid out, the sun was peeking through the large eucalyptus trees. Dappled light reached out to touch the rainbow colors beginning to take shape across the grass. Ist sat down next to an empty space in the quilt. From my carryall I removed the folded three feet by six feet panel, the size of a grave. I smoothed it with a shaking hand, hot tears filling my eyes. *I hope you're seeing this, Joe. Your memory panel is lovely.*

The bright blue poplin background held smaller blocks – one with a bright sun over green fields, another with a mountaintop capped with snow, one with foamy waves crashing on a sandy shore – a depiction of places that Joe had loved to visit. The last corner block held Joe's photograph that had been inserted via an iron-on transfer and sewn onto the block with his name, date of birth and date of death. The center block held an appliquéd dove cut from the fabric of one of Joe's favorite white shirts, an embroidered olive branch in its peak.

I felt the presence of someone before the woman knelt. Her gray head was bowed as she reached out to touch Joe's name. Tears dripped onto the panel and when she raised her eyes to meet mine, I saw Joe in their brown depths. Over the quilt, our hands reached out and clasped tightly.

"May I help?" Her words were a hoarse whisper. "I was weak in the last months of his life. I must not fail him in death."

Together, we lifted the quilted panel and lowered it into place. Joining the thousands of others.

It was a simple piece.

A symbol of one man's life.

A testimony to a struggle that continues.

~

About The Author

Barbara Deming's writing career began at age ten when she climbed up into a mulberry tree with a Red Chief tablet and pencil to compose her first story. Though she no longer climbs trees, her writing appears in such magazines as *Grit, The Storyteller, Rockford Review,* online in *Journal Of The Blue Planet, The Emporium Gazette, and Cenotaph,* plus various newspapers. Her stories have appeared in the book, *Southern Nights: A Mystery & Suspense Collection by Southern Writers* and in *Forget Me Knots...From the Front Porch Anthologies.* Her work has also been nominated for a Pushcart Prize.

When not writing, Barbara leads a writing workshop, does volunteer work at the Joslyn Senior Center and the United Methodist Church, and travels as much as the budget allows. She lives in San Marcos, California, with her husband and a collection of quilts.

~~~~~~~~~~~~~~~~~~~~~~~~~~~~~~~~~~

~ Grateful acknowledgment is made to the following publications in which Barbara's short stories have appeared:

PINWHEELS FOR SALE

The Rockford Review, Spring/Summer 2001

TEDDY BEAR's PICNIC

The Rockford Review, Winter 2001

SUNSHINE AND SHADOWS

GRIT Magazine, January 21, 2001

JACOB'S LADDER

AIM Magazine, Spring 2000

JOSEPH'S COAT

Palomar Showcase, Spring 2000

(Third Place, The National League of Pen Women Contest)

3' X 6'

A&U Magazine, April 2000

~ Barbara Deming,

Contributing Author to: *Forget Me Knots From the Front Porch*, published by Obadiah Press.

Short Stories included in The Book of Angel & Ghost Mysteries, coming May 2003, from Southern Star Publishing

Latest Book: *The Quilt Maker - A Story Collection,* published by Southern Star Publishing

Author's Email: tejasbabs@aol.com

Printed in the United States
1426100001B/118-153

9 781591 094906